AMBUSH BY AN EXPERT

The man with the rifle was good—almost too good to believe. Already Skye Fargo had used every trick he knew to turn the tables on the assassin taking aim at him from ambush—and nothing had worked.

Now—just in time—he spied a bright glimmer of light, the reflection of sunlight off a metal gun barrel. Fargo frantically threw himself to the right. He heard the killer's rifle thunder and felt dirt strike his face as the bullet smacked into the soil.

Swiftly, Skye rolled behind a birch as a slug thudded into the trunk. Hunkering down, he fed a cartridge into his Sharps, cocked the hammer, and set the trigger. So far he had been incredibly lucky. But he couldn't expect his luck to last forever.

Trouble was, he also couldn't expect his foe to make a mistake. For the first time Skye was up against someone as smart and skilled at slaying and survival as he was.

The Trailsman had met his match.

And he just might be about to meet his end. . . .

THE

TRAILSMAN

138

SILVER FURY

by

Jon Sharpe

Ⓞ

A SIGNET BOOK

SIGNET
Published by the Penguin Group
Penguin Books USA Inc., 375 Hudson Street,
New York, New York 10014, U.S.A.
Penguin Books Ltd, 27 Wrights Lane,
London W8 5TZ, England
Penguin Books Australia Ltd, Ringwood,
Victoria, Australia
Penguin Books Canada Ltd, 10 Alcorn Avenue,
Toronto, Ontario, Canada M4V 3B2
Penguin Books (N.Z.) Ltd, 182-190 Wairau Road,
Auckland 10, New Zealand

Penguin Books Ltd, Registered Offices:
Harmondsworth, Middlesex, England

First published by Signet, an imprint of New American Library,
a division of Penguin Books USA Inc.

First Printing, June, 1993
10 9 8 7 6 5 4 3 2 1

The first chapter of this book previously appeared in *Moon Lake Massacre*,
the one hundred thirty-seventh volume in this series.

 REGISTERED TRADEMARK—MARCA REGISTRADA

Printed in the United States of America

The Trailsman

Beginnings . . . they bend the tree and they mark the man. Skye Fargo was born when he was eighteen. Terror was his midwife, vengeance his first cry. Killing spawned Skye Fargo, ruthless, cold-blooded murder. Out of the acrid smoke of gunpowder still hanging in the air, he rose, cried out a promise never forgotten.

The Trailsman they began to call him all across the West: searcher, scout, hunter, the man who could see where others only looked, his skills for hire but not his soul, the man who lived each day to the fullest, yet trailed each tomorrow. Skye Fargo, the Trailsman, the seeker who could take the wildness of a land and the wanting of a woman and make them his own.

1860 . . . in a remote region
of the Rocky Mountains
where the unwary seldom
lived long.

1

Someone was following him.

The big man astride the sure-footed pinto stallion did nothing to betray his awareness of being trailed as he wound his slow way upward along a narrow game trail. Skye Fargo was no stranger to the West; he knew the wild, pristine land better than most, and he knew that those who survived the longest were the ones who never acted rashly. Recklessness was certain suicide, and he aimed to live to a ripe old age and die in bed with a passionate vixen cuddled at his side.

So he kept on riding, sitting loosely in the saddle, his brawny left hand lightly clasping the reins, his lake blue eyes fixed on the pines and aspens lining the trail ahead while his keen ears strained for more telltale sounds from the owl hoot dogging him. It must be someone up to no good, he reasoned, or whoever it was wouldn't be trying so hard to be stealthy—and failing miserably.

Fargo had heard several twigs snap, and once a small stone rattled down the slope on his left, which told him he wasn't being stalked by Indians. No self-respecting warrior would make so much noise. It was a white man, then, and one with little wilderness experience. Even so, the man must be considered highly dangerous. A bullet from a greenhorn's gun was just as deadly as a slug from the six-shooter of a seasoned *pistolero*.

He figured the unknown stalker had been behind him for better than five minutes. Somehow, he must force the man out into the open. At any moment he might be shot in the back, a thought that caused his skin to prickle. Shifting slightly in the saddle, he casually rested his right hand within inches of his Colt.

The trail brought him to the top of a rise where a wide clearing gave him an excuse to rein up and dismount.

9

Fargo deliberately turned the stallion so that he swung down on the far side from the trees where the stalker was concealed. As his right boot touched the ground, he palmed the Colt and held it between his body and the Ovaro. Then he pretended to adjust the cinch while surreptitiously peering out from under the brim of his white hat at the wall of vegetation below.

Something rustled in a dense thicket.

Fargo glimpsed a flash of color, a streak of blue against the backdrop of green. Then a slim figure in a blue homespun shirt and white-tan cotton duck pants appeared, darting from tree to tree, drawing ever closer. Clutched in the man's hands was a rifle. Fargo was ready to throw himself to either side should the man level the gun, but, oddly enough, the greenhorn didn't bother to bring the weapon into play. Instead, holding the barrel vertical, the man raced to the edge of the clearing and abruptly halted.

"Don't make any sudden moves if you value your life, mister!" he bellowed, his brown eyes ablaze with resolve. An unkempt beard covered the lower half of his angular face.

Fargo straightened and touched the hammer of his Colt. All it would take was a flick of his arm upward, and he could drop the man before the greenhorn knew what was happening, but he held his fire. "Howdy, stranger," he said pleasantly. "What can I do for you?"

He looked to be all tuckered out and as skittish as a colt at a branding. Swallowing, he licked his thin lips, and nodded at the stallion. "I need your horse, mister. If you step back and let me take him, there won't be any trouble." He paused and scanned the forest ringing them. "I'm truly sorry about this but I have no choice."

"Horse stealing can get a man hanged in these parts," Fargo said.

"I'm dead anyway if I don't light a shuck," the man said forlornly and broke into a fit of violent coughing. He was clearly ill. His skin was unnaturally pale, and he appeared to have recently lost a great deal of weight. His shabby clothes, which once must have fit, hung on his scarecrow frame in droopy folds. Both boots had holes in them, and one was missing the heel. He wore no hat.

His long black hair, greasy and dishevelled, made him look even more crazy.

"You look like you could use a hot meal and plenty of rest," Fargo commented. "How about if I whip up a pot of fresh coffee?"

Astonishment etched the man's features. "Didn't you hear me?" he demanded, advancing several strides and wagging the rifle. "I need your horse. If you don't get out of the way right this instant, I'm liable to kill you."

"You're not the killing kind."

"What?" the man blurted. "How can you say a thing like that? You don't know me."

"True. But I've run into enough gunmen, renegades, and savages in my time to know a hardened killer when I see one," Fargo said, elevating his arm a bit higher. "If you were really cold-blooded, you would have shot me back on the trail when you were following me."

"You knew I was there?"

"You made more noise than a herd of buffalo," Fargo said. Suddenly he extended his arm over the top of the saddle, trained the Colt on the man's chest, and cocked the hammer. "Now why don't you put down that rifle and we'll talk this over?"

The man stiffened and made as if to point his rifle. One glance at Fargo's face changed his mind and he reluctantly lowered the gun to the ground. "Damn me for being the biggest fool in all creation!" he muttered.

"What's your handle?" Fargo asked, being careful to keep the Colt fixed on the greenhorn as he stepped around the stallion.

"Pitman. Charlie Pitman."

"If you don't mind me saying so, Charlie, you'd better rustle up a new line of work. You sure weren't cut out to be an outlaw."

"I'm no thief!" Pitman bristled. "I was a wrangler before I got a fool notion into my head to see some more of the world." He pressed a palm to his sweaty brow. "If I wasn't so desperate, I'd never, ever do something like this."

"Care to explain?"

Pitman again surveyed the forest, then said nervously, "Gladly, mister. But first we have to hightail it out of here before they show up."

"They?"

"The bastards who are out for my hide. They don't take kindly to someone escaping, and they'll track me down for sure. That Cutler fellow can follow a fox over solid rock, they say."

His curiosity fully aroused, Fargo walked over to pick up Pitman's rifle, then mounted the Ovaro and motioned at the sea of trees to the south of the clearing. "Lead the way. I'll tell you when to stop." He saw relief on the man's face as Pitman turned and entered the cover of the woods. There could be no doubt that Pitman was genuinely scared to death of whoever was after him. Who could it be? And why?

They traveled twenty yards before the scarecrow spoke. "If I make it out of this mess alive, I swear that I'm going back to Ohio and visit my folks. I never should have left home five years ago in the first place."

An irate squirrel, upset by their intrusion into its domain, chattered angrily at them from a high limb.

"Sometimes a fella doesn't realize how good he has things until he loses them," Pitman went on. "If I'd known what was in store for me when I rode off, I'd have stayed put." Once more he mopped his forehead. "But I was younger then. I figured I knew it all. Went to Texas and got me a job on a ranch. It was all right for a spell. Wrangling is hard work, though, and it wears a man down after a while. So I took my pay and headed for Denver. There I got me the idea to go to California." Pitman snorted. "What a jackass!"

Fargo had met many such men in his travels, roamers filled with an unquenchable wanderlust, carefree souls eager to see the many wonders the country had to offer. They drifted from place to place, job to job, always seeking something better over the next horizon. Why there were so many was no great secret. The lure of adventure the untamed land west of the Mississippi River promised drew them like a magnet attracted bits of iron. They could no more resist the call of the wild than they could stop breathing—as he well knew, because he shared their urge to see all there was to see.

As Pitman began relating his childhood in Ohio, Fargo listened with half an ear. The rest of his attention was focused on the sounds and rhythms of the forest. He heard sparrows singing gaily off to the right and the breeze rustling through the pines. The squirrel chattered for a minute, then abruptly ceased.

"—Pa always wanted me to follow in his footsteps and be a farmer," Pitman was saying. "But no! I was too good for that kind of work. You wouldn't catch me plowing a field or feeding slop to a bunch of hungry hogs!" He laughed bitterly. "I thought the life of a farmer was the most boring life in the world. I wanted something better."

"Did you find it?" Fargo asked.

"I sure as hell did not," Pitman said. "Instead I learned that farming is no worse than most other jobs. In fact, it's better. No matter what a man does for a living, he has to work hard at it if he wants to make something of himself."

For over a hundred yards they moved in silence except for the dull clomping of the Ovaro's hoofs.

"Tell me more about these people who are after you," Fargo prompted. He had heard nothing to indicate there was anyone else within miles of where they were, but he still believed the man's story and wanted to learn as much as he could about the situation before anyone showed up.

"When we stop," Pitman said.

The soft gurgling of water drew them to a grassy tract flanking a gently flowing stream. Pitman immediately sank to his knees and gulped greedily, getting his chin and shirt soaking wet. "Lord, this hits the spot! I haven't had a drop to drink since I ran off. That was pretty near twenty-four hours ago."

Fargo wedged the man's rifle into his bedroll, then climbed down and let the stallion drink its fill. He studied his newfound acquaintance, noting the deep lines in Pitman's haggard face and the flecks of gray in the man's greasy hair. Pitman looked to be thirty-five or forty, but Fargo had the impression he was much younger. "If you don't mind me asking, Charlie, how old are you?"

Pitman paused in the act of scooping more water to his mouth. "Twenty-four, but you'd never guess it from the way I look. That's what they did to me. Nine months of hard labor is enough to ruin any man."

"Hard labor?" Fargo repeated. "Were you in prison?"

Pitman looked up and opened his mouth to answer when the stillness around them was shattered by the harsh blast of a gun. At that moment the center of Pitman's forehead burst outward as a slug tore through his head from back to front, showering blood, flesh, and gore all over the grass. Charlie uttered a strangled groan and pitched forward.

Fargo was in motion before the echo of the blast died away. Automatically pinpointing the direction the shot came from, he crouched and whirled toward the undergrowth where the rifleman lurked, his Colt flashing from its holster. He saw telltale wisps of gunsmoke thirty yards away above the dense brush on the other side of the stream and fired three times in swift succession, fanning the revolver and elevating the barrel a hair to compensate for range. Then he lunged at the stallion, grabbed the reins and pulled the pinto into cover behind some pines. In a flash he had the Sharps in his hand and the Colt back on his hip.

An eerie quiet enveloped the forest. All the birds and other wildlife had fallen mute.

Fargo leaned against a trunk and fed a bullet into the Sharps. He glanced once at Charlie Pitman, sprawled limply on the dank earth with a crimson pool forming around his head, before moving on cat's feet toward the water. Had he hit the bushwhacker? Or was the man just waiting out there for the chance to slay him, too?

At the last pine fronting the stream he stopped to scour the forest beyond and gird himself for the next step. He had to cross a narrow strip of grass, vault the stream, and reach the trees beyond. For three or four seconds he would be in the open, exposed and helpless.

Taking a deep breath, Fargo hurtled from behind the trunk, darted to the bank, and leaped. To the southwest a rifle cracked and something nipped at the fringe adorning the left side of his buckskins. Then he landed solidly on both soles, ducked down, and scooted into a tangle of bushes.

Fargo flattened himself and aimed his rifle. There were two triggers on a Sharps: by pulling the rear one, Fargo set the front trigger so that all he had to do was tap it and the rifle would fire. Such a hair trigger came in handy when a man had to shoot in a hurry, when the difference between life and death could be measured in the blink of an eye.

Rising but staying hunched over, he angled to the right. The rifleman had prudently changed position, moving ten yards to the north of where he had been when he shot Pitman. This was no greenhorn. Something told Fargo that he was up against someone skilled at killing.

He used every available cover, his eyes constantly sweeping back and forth, alert for any movement. Whoever was out there was bound to move again and might give himself away. Skirting a thicket, he glided to a fir tree and stopped to get his bearings.

Once more the crisp mountain air shattered in the boom of a large-caliber rifle.

The trunk next to Fargo's cheek exploded in a shower of splinters and bits of woods. Instinctively he dropped down, then sprinted for a large boulder a dozen feet away. Taking a flying dive, he landed on his elbows and knees, jarring his limbs.

His pulse pounded like a tom-tom. That had been too damn close for comfort! he reflected, and rose to his knees. He touched his left hand to his cheek, and when he lowered the hand there were drops of blood on the tips of his first two fingers. If one of those razor-sharp slivers had struck an eye, he'd have been blinded.

The rifleman had changed position again. This time the shot had come from a point fifteen yards to the left of where the killer had been when he fired as Fargo jumped the stream. Fargo knew the man was probably moving once more at that very moment. But which way? If he could outguess the bastard, he'd turn the tables.

He risked a peek over the boulder and nearly lost his head. Stone chips stung his face as a slug scoured a groove close to the tip of his nose, then ricocheted off into the vegetation. Going prone, he crawled into high weeds behind him, slanted to the left, and snaked his way in a loop intended to bring him up on the bushwhacker from the rear.

Suddenly he spotted a vague shape jogging in a beeline to the north. There was a hint of buckskins, and he glimpsed some sort of fur cap. Whipping the Sharps to his shoulder, he took a hasty bead, steadied the barrel, and squeezed off a shot.

15

The man disappeared.

Had he missed? Fargo wondered, hastily inserting a new cartridge. He remembered to move, to put himself somewhere else in case the bushwhacker had pinpointed where he was, and galvanized into motion, sprinting to the right. A fraction of a second after he took his first step, a bullet buzzed through the space his body had just occupied.

The killer was very much alive.

Fargo plunged into shoulder-high brush, plowed a path into the center, and abruptly halted, crouching to catch his wind. Faintly he heard pounding footsteps, then silence. The rifleman had moved again. But where?

Lowering onto his stomach, Fargo removed his hat and held it in his left hand as he swiftly crawled to the west edge of the brush. Dappled by shadows and sparkling beams of sunlight, the forest presented a deceptive picture of tranquility. He searched high and low but saw no sign of the killer. Putting his hat back on, he braced his left hand on the ground and tensed to shove erect when out of the corner of his eye he spied a bright glimmer of light, the reflection of sunlight off a metal gun barrel.

Fargo frantically threw himself to the right. He heard the killer's rifle thunder and felt dirt strike his face as the bullet smacked into the soil. Twisting, he hastily sighted on the tree shielding the mystery rifleman and fired, doubting he would score but hoping to give the killer pause long enough for himself to reach safety.

Springing up, Fargo ran and ducked behind a spruce. Another shot blasted, the slug thudding into the trunk. Hunkering down, he fed a fresh cartridge into the Sharps, cocked the hammer, and set the trigger. So far he had been incredibly lucky, but he couldn't expect his luck to last forever. Either he figured a way to end the fight and end it quickly, or he'd wind up like Charlie Pitman.

Fargo had to hand it to the killer. The man was as good as they came, as good as *he* was, even—an equal, someone with as much experience as he had, someone whose skill set him apart from the ordinary frontiersman. Such men were not all that common. Kit Carson, Jim Bridger, Joe Walker, and a dozen or so others were equally renowned, but they were men of great personal integrity, not the kind to shoot someone from ambush. The man he was up against had to be a scout or mountain man gone bad.

Fargo had met most of the more famous frontiersmen at one time or another. And those he hadn't met, he'd heard about. Small wonder, since the favorite pastime in every saloon and tavern in the settlements and around every campfire on the Oregon Trail and other routes west was the sharing of the latest news concerning the exploits of men who deservedly earned widespread reputations. Intrepid explorers like Bridger and Walker and adventurers like Carson were household names.

So, too, was the name of the Trailsman, though Fargo had never asked for the title. Somewhere along the line someone came up with it and the name stuck. Now, wherever he went, that was how he was known. Not that he minded. Troublemakers were less inclined to tangle with someone rumored to eat live grizzlies for breakfast.

Now, as Fargo scanned the woods on all sides, he wondered if he knew the man trying to kill him or whether he had heard about him. The odds were he had. It made no difference, though. He would shoot the son of a bitch dead the minute he got a clear shot, and that would be that.

A minute passed. Two. Vigilant as a hawk, Fargo scrutinized every shadow, surveyed every possible hiding place, but spied no one. Immobile as a rock, he waited for the killer to make a mistake, but the man never did. After five minutes of absolute quiet, he took a gamble. Squatting, he picked up a small stone, then threw it with all his might.

The stone struck a fir tree and clattered to the earth.

Fargo had the Sharps tucked to his shoulder, ready to fire. But there was no reaction from the killer. The man didn't fall for the ploy and snap off a shot in the direction of the sound, as Fargo had hoped. Perhaps the killer was gone, he speculated. Yet it wouldn't do to step out into the open, not until he was certain.

For ten more minutes he stayed where he was. Finally several sparrows flitted through the trees across the way, singing merrily as they frolicked. A jay, betraying no alarm, alighted in a nearby pine. He saw a butterfly fluttering through the undergrowth. The wild creatures were

17

resuming their interrupted lives, which meant all was well.

Still, Fargo proceeded cautiously. He conducted a search of the area and found clear tracks in the soft soil at the base of a tree. They were moccasin prints, and they revealed the killer to weigh two hundred pounds or better, judging by their depth. Working outward from the tree, he found where the man had run off, going to the east.

Giving chase would be pointless. The killer had a five-to ten-minute head start and must be a mile off already. More, if the man had a horse hidden nearby.

Fargo contented himself with examining the ground for more footprints. A competent tracker could tell a lot from the tracks a person made. In this case, based on the way the killer had moved with his toes pointed slightly inward, Fargo deduced the bushwhacker might be part Indian because white men invariably walked with their toes pointed outward.

Fargo's hunch was confirmed by the shape of the tracks themselves. No two Indian tribes made their moccasins the same way; the shapes of the heels and the toes were always unique with each one. The Crows, for instance, wore moccasins that curved from the heel to the toe. Pawnees wore moccasins with exceptionally wide soles, whereas Kiowas preferred moccasins with narrow toes.

The tracks he found bore slender heels and wide toes. Those were the earmarks of Arapaho moccasins. So it was possible the killer had spent a lot of time with that tribe. He straightened, his brow knit in thought. A fuzzy recollection nipped at the back of his mind, something he had heard once about a mountain man living with the Arapahos, but he couldn't remember the whole story.

Shrugging, Fargo headed for the stream. He would have to bury Pitman. Then what? Should he press on westward as he had been doing when the greenhorn appeared, or should he try to track down the killer? Unable to decide, he waded into the shallow water and walked past Pitman's corpse. At the pines beyond he stopped, rage flaring within him.

The Ovaro was gone.

2

The tracks told the whole story.

While Fargo had been waiting for the killer to show himself, the crafty bushwhacker had circled around and taken the stallion. Fargo saw that the man had been leading the Ovaro instead of riding, a smart move since the pinto was likely to buck if a stranger climbed aboard. He began running, easily following the hoof prints, afraid of what he would find.

Several hundred yards from the stream he came to a small clearing where a tethered horse had been waiting. The man had mounted, then ridden to the north with the stallion in tow. "Damn!" he muttered and slapped his thigh in frustration. The killer had made a fool of him, plain and simple.

Fargo took a stride, then hesitated, looking over his shoulder toward the stream. As much as he wanted to do the proper thing by Pitman, he dared not waste precious time. The coyotes, buzzards, and other scavengers would see to Pitman's remains. He had to retrieve the Ovaro.

Shrugging, Fargo resumed his pursuit. Sooner or later the killer would stop. Barring heavy rains, Fargo would stick to the trail until he overtook the horse thief and settled accounts.

Although most men would shudder at the thought of being stranded on foot in the Rocky Mountains, he wasn't worried about surviving. Besides the Colt and the Sharps, he had a throwing knife, a keen-edged Arkansas toothpick, snug in a leather sheath tucked inside his right boot. Slaying game would be no problem. And finding water was no worry, either. He knew how to read the lay of the land, how to figure out where the low-lying streams and creeks were most likely to be. If he had to, he could remove his shirt and use it at first light to mop dew up off the grass. By wringing the shirt over a makeshift bark bowl, he'd collect enough water to keep him going.

To the west snow glistened on towering peaks. To the east lay the green foothills bordering the windswept prairie. Under ordinary circumstances Fargo would have admired the beauty of the rugged landscape, but now all he could think about was the dependable Ovaro. He'd been through a lot with that horse, and it had seldom let him down. Like many a man who spent most of his days in the saddle, he'd grown strongly attached to the pinto. It had become more friend than mere animal. If anything happened to it, he'd make the killer sorry he was ever born.

Anger fueled the fast pace he set. The Sharps cradled in the crook of his left arm, he hiked mile after mile until the sun was poised directly overhead. Then, in the welcome shade of a mighty evergreen, he sat with his back against the trunk and contemplated his predicament.

He must be careful not to overexert himself. Working up a sweat at high altitudes was deceptively dangerous because the cool layer of perspiration kept the body temperature low, and if the temperature fell too low, you'd die. Many a trapper, back when white men first flocked to the mountains after prime beaver pelts, had learned the hard way.

He continued walking. He was puzzled by the direction the killer was taking. There was nothing to the north but more mountains and a near limitless expanse of forest. The region was so remote that whites seldom visited it. The trappers had, of course, decades ago. And more recently, ten or eleven years back, there had been a frequently used trail just to the south, a trail that had taken gold-hungry Easterners to California during the great rush of '49. But the frenzied exodus of greed-driven souls had long since died out.

The new gold fields were located in the majestic mountains west of Denver. In the past year Denver had grown from a small speck on the map to a full-fledged city with all the trappings of cultured society. Theaters, bawdy houses, and gambling dens lined street after street. It was a wild town where practically anything was tolerated.

The last time he had been there, he barely got out with his life.

By Fargo's reckoning, Denver lay ninety to a hundred miles to the southeast. He would have expected the killer to head in that direction, if for no other reason than to sell the Ovaro for top dollar. The stallion was a fine horse. Anyone who knew horseflesh would jump at the chance to own it.

The afternoon faded, but then brilliant streaks of pink and orange tinged the western sky when the sun touched the horizon. In the distance a coyote yipped. As often happened at that time of the day, the wind picked up, rustling the trees and the grass.

Fargo sought shelter for the night in a gully. While gathering dry wood for a fire, he happened to spot a rabbit huddled under a bush. Soundlessly he leaned down and drew the toothpick. Holding the tip of the blade in his fingers, he gauged the range, then stamped his foot and shouted. Predictably the rabbit shot out from under the bush, bounded a few yards, then paused to stare at him. It was then he hurled the knife, his body a blur, his concentration total.

The blade caught the rabbit squarely in the belly, and the creature leaped straight into the air.

A crackling fire and a hearty supper of deliciously roasted meat did wonders to restore Fargo's vitality. He cut some of the rabbit into strips and hung them on sticks to dry overnight so he would have something to eat the next day. Then, after preparing a soft bed of grass and pine needles at the base of the gully wall, he stretched out on his side, placed the Sharps in front of him, and went instantly to sleep.

Dawn found Fargo well on his way. The killer had shunned the high ground, which made the going easier. Two hours of travel brought him to a creek where he drank his fill. Charred embers showed this was where the bushwhacker had stopped for the night. He wasn't all that far behind, which surprised him. The killer should be covering ground swiftly, not taking his time about getting to wherever he was headed.

Fargo chalked up the bushwhacker's slow pace to over-confidence and outright carelessness. The man must figure he had gotten safely away. Fargo knew he would prove him wrong soon enough.

Until noon he followed a winding course among the mountains and hills, never once losing the sign. Shod hoofs left plenty of spoor, even on hard-packed soil. He found where the killer had gone to the top of the ridge, apparently to scan the countryside, then ridden northward again. Had he been spotted? He doubted it because the tracks were plainly those of walking horses. Surely, if the bushwhacker had seen him, the man would now be galloping off for parts unknown.

Fargo's legs began to ache, but he ignored the discomfort. The exercise would do him good. Sometimes he spent too much time on the stallion—at the expense of his stamina.

By midafternoon he had finished the last piece of rabbit and his growling stomach was reminding him he should find something else to eat. He rounded a hill, then halted in amazement, confounded by the sight of a wide trail bearing the tracks of many horses. Some were old prints, others new. Among them were those of the Ovaro, which he knew as well as he did his own facial features. The killer had angled to the left, taking this new trail to the northwest.

Mystified, Fargo sank to one knee and pondered. Obviously people used this trail regularly. But where did it lead? To the northwest was nothing but unmapped wilderness. It made no sense whatsoever for there to be a well-used trail smack in the middle of nowhere. Scanning the ground, he noticed wagon-wheel ruts, further contributing to the puzzle.

There was only one way to find the answer. Rising, he walked on. The trail led him between a pair of peaks, each capped by spires of stone that resembled nothing so much as twin oversized tepees. Once past the mountains the trail entered a gorge. And there, nailed to a tree at the gorge mouth, was another discovery that stopped him in his tracks.

"What the hell?" Fargo said to himself and moved up to the tree to examine the crudely painted sign, years old, that bore three faded words: WELCOME TO SERENITY. He touched the cracked wood and shook his head in disbelief. There couldn't possibly be a town nearby. If there was, he'd have heard of it. Yet there was the sign, proving him wrong.

Cradling the Sharps, he slowly entered the gorge. On both sides towered sheer rock walls. The dirt underfoot was scarred by countless hoofprints of horses coming and going. The wagon ruts revealed that heavily laden wagons had also gone both ways on numerous occasions.

Abruptly the gorge ended, widening out into a fertile valley ringed by high mountains. In the distance, about two miles away, Fargo could see buildings.

He halted and received yet another shock. Tied to a tree not fifty yards away, close to the trail leading to the town, was his stallion! Suspecting that the Ovaro had been intentionally left there as a lure to draw him into an ambush, he leveled the rifle and warily advanced. Strangely there was no movement among the trees, no sign at all of anything out of the ordinary. He kept expecting to hear the crack of a shot, but all he heard was the whispering breeze and the chirping of a robin. Without mishap he reached the Ovaro's side.

Lowering the Sharps, Fargo scratched his bearded chin. Seldom had he ever been as confused as now. Why would the killer leave the stallion there, then go off? It was crazy, yet that was exactly what the man had done as the tracks showed. The bushwhacker had tied the Ovaro's reins to a low limb and headed for the town.

Fargo checked his bedroll and saddlebags. All of his possessions were there. Not a single article had been stolen. He ran his hands over the pinto, paying particular attention to its legs and hoofs, but found nothing wrong with the shoes and no evidence the horse had gone lame. There was no reason for the killer to have left it behind.

Thoroughly confounded, Fargo slid the Sharps into the saddle scabbard and climbed up. He remembered where the killer had gone to the top of a ridge to look around, and he wondered again if the man had seen him and subsequently decided to leave the stallion for him to find. But the notion was ridiculous. The killer could have easily gone on until rain obliterated all the tracks, leaving him free to do with the stallion as he wished without fear of being eventually caught. Besides, no one in his right mind stole a horse one day and returned it to the owner the next. There had to be another explanation.

Perhaps he would find it in Serenity.

Turning the pinto, Fargo followed the rutted track toward the mystery town. Would he find the killer there? He hadn't gotten a good look but he was certain he would know the man when he laid eyes on him. And when he did, there would be hell to pay. He checked his Colt to make sure it was loaded, gave the cylinder a spin, and twirled the revolver back into his holster. The Arkansas toothpick was in place inside his boot.

Wide tracts of grass now bordered the trail. He saw a few dozen head of cattle grazing contentedly and marveled that someone had brought the beef to the remote site. Farther on he spied a small herd of horses. Whoever had gone to so much trouble in bringing the animals to the valley evidently planned to stay for a long time.

When he grew close enough, he counted seven buildings strung out in a line from north to south. Past them, a quarter of a mile or less, loomed a dark, forboding mountain. A few horses were tied to hitching posts, and faintly on the sultry breeze came the tinny sound of piano music.

Fargo racked his brain but he could recollect no reference to the town. The buildings, he now saw, were in run-down condition. Like the sign back at the gorge, they had been crudely built. All needed painting, and some of the roofs were in need of immediate repair. From the largest structure, a square building occupying the center of the row, arose the music. As he angled toward the hitching post in front of the bat-wing doors, he heard gruff voices and female laughter.

Reining up, he looked both ways and saw no one. A large mongrel dog glanced at him but displayed no interest or alarm. The two horses already at the hitching post stood with their heads drooping, dozing in the heat of the sun. Serenity, he decided, certainly lived up to its name.

Sliding down, Fargo secured the Ovaro to the post, shucked the Sharps, and strolled to the bat-wing doors where he stopped to survey the interior and give his eyes time to adjust to the dim light within.

A bar ran along the rear wall. Two men were drinking at one end, while talking to the barkeep and a young lovely in a tight red dress. To the left were three card tables, and at one three men sat, playing poker. To the right was a long table of the type commonly found in restaurants. Close to it stood the piano where a man in a bowler sat tapping the keys.

Fargo shoved the doors wide and ambled inside. Everyone in the room stopped what they were doing to glance around and take his measure. He walked straight to the bar, deposited the Sharps with a loud thump, and nodded at the bartender.

The barkeep was a portly, bald man wearing a white apron over his clothes. He also wore a wide smile. "Howdy, stranger. What's your poison?"

"Whiskey," Fargo said.

"Coming right up," the bartender said, moving to a shelf of liquor bottles. "My name is Griswald, by the way. I own this place. If you're hungry, I can go in back and whip you up a steak and potatoes. Or if you're of a mind for cards, I'm sure the boys at the table will oblige you."

"I may take you up on that food in a while," Fargo said, "but right now all I want to do is wet my whistle."

"This must be your first time in town," Griswald commented casually as he poured the whiskey. "I know I've never seen you around before in the ten years I've owned this place." He grinned. "I have a good memory for faces. Never forget a one."

"Is that how long the town has been here? Ten years?"

"More like twelve," Griswald replied, placing the bottle down. "You sound surprised."

"I've never heard of it."

"Most folks haven't. It's a bit off the beaten path."

"It's a *lot* off the beaten path," Fargo corrected him, and downed the whiskey in a single gulp. He felt the burning liquid's fiery path down his throat.

"That's why I like Serenity so much," Griswald said, resting his elbows on the inner edge of the bar. "A man can take life easy here. There's none of the hustle and bustle you find in the big cities."

"How many folks live here?"

"Oh, let me see," Griswald said, his forehead furrowing as he mentally counted them off, "there's me and the two girls, Gloria and Shirley, and there's the ten who work for Mr. Traute, who pretty much owns the valley, and there's the marshal—"

"Serenity has a marshal?" Fargo interrupted and smiled at the idea of such a small, backwater town having its own law officer. "What's he do? Keep the dog from becoming too rowdy on Saturday nights?"

Griswald chuckled. "Not exactly. Mainly he spends his time sitting in his office with his feet propped on his desk and his hat pulled down over his eyes so no one can see he's sleeping."

Shifting, Fargo studied each of the men. None wore buckskins or an unusual hat. "Has anyone else come in here within the past hour or two?"

"Not a soul. Why? Are you looking for someone?"

"I sure as hell am," Fargo said and handed over the glass for a refill. Not one of the horses outside had appeared to have been ridden hard during the morning, which convinced him the bushwhacker must be elsewhere, perhaps in another building. "Is there a livery in Serenity?"

"Of sorts. There's a barn at the far end that serves for boarding stock. Jeeter there runs it," Griswald said, nodding at the piano player. "You have to fork your own hay and rub your animals down yourself, but he does supply some oats if you pay extra."

"Obliged," Fargo said, taking his drink and the Sharps and walked over to the piano. Jeeter looked up, his bloodshot eyes dulled by too much hard liquor.

"Don't tell me, stranger," he said, slurring his words. "I couldn't help but overhear. You want to board your horse."

"I want to know if anyone else has boarded one this morning," Fargo said.

"No, sir. Hell, I ain't had a paying customer in a month or more. Which is why you find me playing this pitiful excuse for a piano to earn my firewater," Jeeter responded, and cackled at some private joke.

Fargo took a sip of whiskey, pondering his next move, when soft footfalls to his rear heralded a smooth arm slipping around his own. Cheap perfume tingled his nose. He gazed into the sparkling brown eyes of the woman in the red dress. She showed a row of even white teeth and

26

raked him with a frank stare that lingered ever so slightly at a spot a few inches below his belt buckle.

"Hello, big man," she greeted him huskily. "I'm Shirley." She put a hand on his shoulder and squeezed, then whistled softly. "My, aren't you the mountain of muscle. I think my prayers have just been answered!"

"Can I buy you a drink?"

"Now aren't you the perfect gentleman," Shirley said, steering him to the long table. Over her shoulder she barked, "Griswald, bring a bottle. And not that rotgut, either. Bring us the real thing."

As Fargo sat down, he noticed one of the men at the bar, eyeing him resentfully. The instant he did, the man promptly looked away.

"So what's your handle?" Shirley asked while crossing her shapely legs. She arranged her dress so that her smooth skin was exposed all the way up to her knees.

Fargo told her.

"Are you fixing to stay long?" Shirley inquired and leaned forward to grin lecherously and wink. "I hope so. I can make it well worth your while."

"I bet you can."

"Anything you want, I'll do. I always aim to please."

"What I want most is information. Do you happen to know a man who wears buckskins and a fur hat?"

Shirley's grin vanished. She seemed to stiffen, then she put a hand to her mouth and coughed. "Buckskins, you say?" Her grin returned. "Honey, the only man in buckskins I've laid eyes on in quite some time is you. And I must say that you are quite an eyeful. They grow 'em handsome in your family, don't they?"

Griswald with the bottle and two glasses gave Fargo an excuse to avoid answering. Shirley's behavior when he mentioned the killer convinced him she knew more than she was admitting. Somehow he must get her to talk. He poured for both of them and took a swallow.

"If I'm not your type, there's another girl who works here who might be," she remarked. "Gloria's older, but she's a thoroughbred where it counts the most."

"I'll keep that in mind," Fargo said and bobbed his head at the card players. "Who might they be?"

"Some of the men who work for Mr. Traute," Shirley said. She pointed at the pair at the bar. "The same with them. When they're not working they hang around here. Hell, there's not much else for them to do in this godforsaken valley."

"If you feel that way, why do you stay?"

For a moment Shirley's face showed intense emotion. A second later it evaporated, and she was all smiles. "A girl has to eat, doesn't she?"

"You could eat just as well, if not better, in Denver. Someone as good looking as you would have no trouble making ends meet," Fargo said. He was startled to see tears begin to form in her eyes. She blinked, bowed her head, and sighed. "Did I say something wrong?" he asked.

"No," she said in a strained tone. Then she shook her head, swirling her long brown hair, and looked up, beaming. "I'm just getting over a wicked cold, and I'm not yet up to snuff." She paused. "One of these days I'll make it to Denver. Or maybe St. Louis. I was born there, you see, and I've always wanted to go back."

"What's stopping you?"

"Nothing."

He didn't believe her. Something was making her miserable. Was Griswald keeping her there against her will? He doubted it. The barkeep didn't impress him as the type. So there must be another reason. "If you want," he offered, "I'll escort you safely to Denver when I leave. You can catch a stage east from there."

"You'd do that for me? You hardly know me."

Now it was Fargo's turn to smile. "By tomorrow morning we can be the best of friends."

Delightful laughter burst from her rosy lips, and she reached out to place a hand on his wrist. "Big man, you don't know how tempted I am."

Fargo leaned back, admiring the swell of her full breasts against the fabric of her dress. She promised to be an armful. By way of making small talk he idly inquired, "What can you tell me about Traute, the man who runs the valley?"

From behind him a low, raspy voice growled, "I don't know about her, mister, but I can tell you he doesn't much like saddle tramps stickin' their noses where they don't belong. Maybe I should shorten yours a mite so you'll know better next time."

3

Fargo heard Shirley's sharp intake of breath as he shifted in his chair to stare at the speaker, a bantam rooster of a man dressed all in black and wearing two pearl-handled pistols in holsters that were tied down for a fast draw. Instead of boots, the man wore moccasins, which explained how he had entered the saloon without Fargo hearing him. The man had a cruel face accented by a nasty scar on his left cheek, a pencil-thin mustache on his upper lip, and beady brown eyes. His mouth was set in a mocking smirk.

All activity in the saloon had ceased, everyone riveted to the tableau at the long table.

"Didn't you hear me, saddle tramp?" the man asked after five seconds went by and Skye had not replied. "Or are you just yellow?"

Fargo made no move for either his Colt or the Sharps. He was at a distinct disadvantage being seated, while the man in black was poised to draw. He said with disdain, "I heard you, mister. But I make it a habit never to waste my time talking to idiots."

Livid with indignation, the man in black impulsively took a step nearer the chair, putting himself in arm's reach, and snarled, "I'm going to kill you, you mangy son of a—"

Fargo's streaking left fist cut the sentence short. His knuckles slammed into the short man's jaw and sent him flying backward into one of the unoccupied card tables. Table and gunman went down in a tumble. Surging upright, Fargo ran over and was ready when the man, sputtering and cursing, came up off the floor in a rush. The gunman realized Fargo was there and made a grab for his guns, trying to draw ambidextrously, using both hands at once.

29

Fargo was not in a charitable mood. Frontier toughs like this were as common as flies and just as troublesome, and Fargo had run into such men time and again, each instance only rankling him more. So when the gunman made a play for his pistols, Fargo waded into the man with his fists flying. His right sank into the gunman's gut, doubling him in half. A left hook lifted him clean off his feet. Two more lightening punches drove the man back against the side wall where he feebly clawed at his guns.

Taking two swift strides, Fargo delivered a kick to the gunman's stomach and the man sank to his knees, spittle dribbling over his lower lip. Planting himself, Fargo gauged the angle and threw all of his weight into a final blow to the man's mouth that left him as flat as a board and out to the world.

"Well done, sir. Well done, indeed."

Two more men had entered during the fight. One wore a fine suit and a large white hat, the other a badge.

"No one has ever bested Mr. Ringald before, sir," said the newcomer in the immaculate brown suit. "I'm afraid he will not take kindly to being thrashed." He smiled at Fargo, his florid features showing no trace of hostility. "But then, it's obvious that you don't much care one way or the other what Mr. Ringald thinks." Extending his right hand he came forward. "Allow me to introduce myself. I'm Vincent Traute."

The man's handshake was firm, his manner cordial. Fargo glanced at the lawman, then back again. "Does Ringald work for you?"

"Yes, I'm sorry to say. He does." Traute lowered his hand and cast a reproachful gaze on the unconscious gunman. "Ringald is my foreman. Having him around is like having a sidewinder for a pet, but even a rattlesnake serves a purpose in the greater scheme of things."

Shirley had risen and walked over. "It wasn't the big man's fault, Mr. Traute," she said anxiously. "Ringald started trouble, just like always."

"That's the truth," Griswald threw in from the bar. "I saw the whole thing. The stranger was just sitting there, minding his own business, when Ringald tore into him."

Traute sighed and pushed his hat back on his head, exposing thick sandy hair. "That's the trouble with sidewinders. They strike even when you don't want them to." Looking at Fargo, he said sincerely, "My apologies, sir, for what has transpired. Ringald has done this sort of thing before, so I know how he can be."

"Then why don't you fire him?" Fargo asked, rubbing the sore knuckles of his right hand.

"Perhaps one day," Traute said. He turned to the lawman. "Ward, would you be so kind as to take Mr. Ringald down to your office and hold him there until I arrive? And be sure to take his toys away from him before he revives, or he just might shoot you out of sheer spite."

Marshal Ward nodded. He was a slovenly sort, his clothes overdue for a washing, a three-day growth of whiskers on his oval chin. A gesture at the three card players brought them over. "Pick him up, boys, and bring him along," Ward directed.

Fargo watched them leave, then went over to the long table and sat down. He was raising his glass when Traute stepped into view on his right.

"Mind if I join you, sir?"

"Suit yourself," Fargo said, emptying the glass in a single swallow.

"Since Ringald is in my employ, I would like to make amends for his unseemly behavior," Traute said, taking a seat. "Allow me to pay for your drinks and anything else you might want while you're in Serenity."

"That's not necessary."

"It's the least I can do."

"I pay my own way," Fargo insisted. Despite Traute's overture, he didn't much like the man. There was something about Traute, a slick air of friendliness much like the phony attitude of a patent medicine salesman, that rubbed Fargo the wrong way.

"As you wish. But don't say I didn't make the offer," Traute said, folding his hands in front of him. He motioned at Griswald, then waited until the bartender arrived before saying, "Tell you what, though, stranger. Why not permit me to make your stay easier by instructing Mr. Griswald here, and Mr. Nestor over at the general store, to let you run up a tab as high as you like? Then you can pay for everything all at once when you leave."

"I'll pay as I go along," Fargo said.

31

"Please," Traute said. "I don't want you to leave our fair valley thinking poorly of our hospitality."

Although strongly tempted to refuse, Fargo pegged Traute as a man accustomed to getting his own way. Refusal would only make Traute more persistent. "If that's what you want, it's fine by me."

"Excellent!" Traute declared, smiling. "I feel better already." Looking at the barkeep, he said, "You heard the man, Mr. Griswald. I hold you responsible for keeping an accurate account of his tab. And I'll tell Nestor to keep you informed of any purchases this man makes so you can add them to the tally, too. Then present the bill when our new friend leaves."

"I understand perfectly, sir," Griswald said.

Fargo stared at Traute with renewed interest. "You own this saloon."

"And the general store. And everything else in Serenity."

"I was told Jeeter runs the livery."

"He runs it for me. Just like Griswald runs the saloon and Nestor the store. Truth to tell, I own the entire valley, lock, stock, and barrel."

"I'm surprised you can make ends meet," Fargo commented. "From what I've seen, you don't get much business here."

An enigmatic smile was Traute's response. Standing, he brushed a piece of lint from his sleeve. "It's been a pleasure meeting you, stranger. Mr. Griswald will now see to all your needs. Good day." He gazed at the two men at the bar. "I expect you back at the ranch in an hour, Burke."

"We'll be there, boss," said the man who had given Fargo the dirty look earlier.

With a nod and a cheery wave, Vincent Traute spun on his heel and marched from the saloon.

Fargo stared thoughtfully at the swinging bat-wing doors. In effect Traute was lord and master of the entire valley. Everyone bowed to his will. But why should a forceful domineering man like Traute, who no doubt had the ability to carve out an empire anywhere in the country, be content with being top dog in such a two-bit dump heap like Serenity? There must be more to the place than met the eye. Or possibly Traute was one of those men who valued privacy above all else, and to whom a place like Serenity would perfectly satisfy his lust for power.

"I'll start that tab now, sir," Griswald announced, taking a pad and pencil from a pocket in his apron. "Trust me. I won't overcharge you."

"You'd better not," Fargo said.

The barkeep departed and was replaced by Shirley, who put a warm hand on Fargo's shoulder and rubbed against his side. "How about another drink, big man? My innards went cold as ice when Ringald braced you."

Fargo poured for her. She sat down beside him and looped her arm in his.

"I should warn you, handsome," she said. "Ringald ain't the type to forgive and forget. No matter what Mr. Traute tells him, he's likely to come gunning for you. You'd better be careful."

"I will."

She sipped her whiskey, rolled it on her tongue, and gave a satisfied "Ahhhh!" after she downed it. "You don't have to worry none about your back, though. Ringald is a low-down murdering bastard, but he has his own code of honor, if you can call it that. He's not a bushwhacker. When he comes after you, he'll call you out and give you a chance to make your play."

Now that was interesting, Fargo reflected. He'd already decided the pint-sized Ringald couldn't have been the man who killed Charlie Pitman since the killer had been much heavier.

"Ringald doesn't have to back shoot," Shirley went on. "He's fast, mister. The fastest I've ever seen, and I've witnessed a few gunfights in my time." She touched Fargo's cheek. "I hope you're as good with that Colt of yours as you are with your fists."

"I'm still alive," Fargo said.

Shirley laughed and raised her glass in a salute. "I'll drink to that, lover. Now why don't you and I wet our whistles a time or three, and if you're lucky, I'll let you walk me to my room later?"

Much later, as it turned out.

They leisurely polished off the bottle, Fargo taking care of the larger share. Halfway through he ordered a steak and potatoes for both of them and was pleased to receive a juicy cut of beef over two inches thick. Toast and butter completed the meal.

The more Shirley drank, the looser her tongue became. She told him all about her childhood, about how her parents had both died and she had been taken to live with an uncle who later imposed himself upon her. She ran away, only to wind up walking the streets in St. Louis. A madam took her in, and soon she was earning more in a month than most people earned in a year.

Along came Vincent Traute. He was in St. Louis on business and stopped at the bawdy house. Shirley caught his eye. Soon the smooth-tongued devil convinced her to return to Serenity with him. Traute promised to take care of her and hinted she would live at his ranch. Instead, she joined Gloria in working at the saloon.

Fargo had heard similar stories many times from women who, through no fault of their own, wound up on the wrong side of the tracks. Though polite society shunned them, they were the salt of the earth—fallen doves, as they were called, who put on no airs like high and mighty rich women.

It was late afternoon before Skye excused himself and took the stallion to the barn at the end of the dusty street. Not a soul stirred anywhere, although loud voices came from the marshal's office. The dog was now lying inside the barn, but it paid no attention to him. He stripped off the saddle and blanket and housed the stallion in a stall, then forked in enough hay to last it awhile. Leaving the saddle draped over the top of the stall, he shouldered his bedroll and saddlebags and walked back to the saloon.

He had the feeling eyes were on him all the way. At the bat-wing doors he paused to scan the buildings, but saw only empty windows. Stepping within, he stopped on seeing the marshal seated at the long table, across from Shirley.

"Don't mind me," Ward said right away. "I just wanted to let you know that Ringald left town with Mr. Traute awhile ago. I heard Mr. Traute tell him not to bother you again or Ringald would regret it. So you can breathe a little easier, mister."

"Thanks," Fargo said, stepping to the table.

"Thank Mr. Traute, not me. He's the one looking out

for your best interests." Ward stood and hooked his thumbs in his gunbelt. "I'll have to keep an eye out in case Ringald tries to sneak back into town, so I'd be obliged if you can tell me how long you plan to stay?"

"I don't rightly know."

"You'll be here overnight, though?"

Fargo glanced at Shirley, who tittered. "Looks that way," he admitted.

"Fair enough. If you have any trouble, I'll come running. Have a good night." Ward tipped his hat, then left.

The bartender joined them, a new bottle of whiskey in his right hand. "Shirley said you'd be wanting this," he stated. "Don't worry about paying me now. It'll go on your tab."

"Give that to me," Shirley said lightheartedly. She grabbed the whiskey and nodded at the entrance. "Come on, I'll show you where I live."

A small two-story building at the north end of town was reserved for the two women. Shirley had the downstairs, her friend Gloria the upstairs. At Shirley's insistence, Traute had ordered that leaks in the roof be repaired and cracks in the wall sealed. And, after considerable nagging, Traute had furnished her place with a few niceties: a worn rug, a stove so she could do her own cooking, and a quilt for her bed.

"I'm sorry you haven't met Gloria yet. She's a lot of fun," Shirley mentioned as she closed the door behind them. "The poor dear is probably worn out after last night. She was busy with one of Traute's men until almost dawn. I expect she'll show up at the saloon by this evening."

Fargo stowed his gear in a corner and sat down. "I've been meaning to ask you," he said. "Have you ever met a man named Charlie Pitman?"

Shirley had gone to a cupboard and removed two glasses. On hearing Pitman's name, stark fear flickered across her face, and one of the glasses slipped from her hand and fell onto the rug. Quickly she stooped and picked it up. "Look at me! All that whiskey has turned me into a butterfingers." She giggled self-consciously.

"You know him, I take it?"

"Yes, as a matter of fact, I do. And I like him a lot.

A whole lot. Charlie used to come into the saloon every now and then, but he hasn't been in for a long time."

"I'm afraid I have some bad news for you, Shirley. Charlie Pitman is dead."

She froze and blanched, her arm outstretched in the act of placing the glasses on a table. "Dear Lord!" she breathed and closed her eyes. "Are you sure?"

"I saw him die. He was shot."

"Who did it?"

"The man I'm hunting, the one I asked you about, the one wearing buckskins and a fur hat."

The glasses clinked together as she slowly set them down. She stepped over to the sole window and gazed blankly out, then mechanically smoothed her dress and brushed at her hair. "I'm sorry to hear that about poor Charlie. I truly am." Her voice broke but she recovered. "Where did this happen?"

"Quite a ways south of here."

Shirley nodded. "Good. Then he made it out for a while, at least."

"Out of where?"

"Out of—" Shirley began, and caught herself, as if abruptly aware of what she was saying. "—out of the valley. He was spending too much time in Serenity, and all because of me."

"I thought you just said he only came by every now and then?" Fargo reminded her, convinced more than ever that she was hiding crucial information. He was determined to uncover the truth and decided the best way would be to earn her trust and friendship.

"Is that what I said?" Shirley responded. She came toward him and laughed gaily. "Don't pay any attention to me, handsome. I babble like a biddy hen when I've had too much to drink. Half the time I don't even know what I'm talking about."

"Then maybe you shouldn't have any more whiskey."

"I think you're right." She stopped directly in front of him, then leaned forward, her red lips hovering close above his mouth. "I'd rather have something else anyway."

Fargo chuckled. "Such as?" he teased and felt his manhood twitch when she ardently kissed him. Her lips were exquisitely soft, her tongue as smooth as silk when she probed his mouth. He brought both hands up and cupped her twin mounds. Her nipples, already hard, pressed into his palms.

"Mmmmmm, nice," Shirley said softly when she broke the kiss. "I knew you'd know how to fire a lady up."

"I'm just getting started," Fargo assured her.

Straightening, her face aglow with impish delight, she took hold of his left hand and tugged him up out of the chair. "We should get nice and comfortable before we get to the main event."

Her bedroom was small and yet nicely furnished with a neatly made bed and a polished chest of drawers, both past their prime.

"This place isn't much, but it's the only home I've got," Shirley remarked, halting next to the bed. Tilting her chin invitingly, she coquettishly clasped her hands behind her back and swayed seductively from side to side. "Show me what you're made of, handsome."

Fargo embraced her and locked his mouth on hers. Her warm breath tingled his nostrils and his hands commenced exploring her voluptuous body, roaming over the full contours of her buttocks to the small of her back and from there around to the front of her thighs. She squirmed deliciously and cooed deep in her throat.

Between her legs was a furnace. His fingers slid along her nether crack, feeling the heat through her dress and underthings. A few pumps of his hand made her gasp and grind against his legs. His organ made a prominent bulge in his pants.

Without warning Skye scooped her into his arms and lowered her onto the bed. She saw the bulge and grinned wickedly, then reached out to trace a finger down the length of his manhood. Fargo removed his gunbelt and his boots, then positioned himself beside her.

"Is there a tree in your britches or are you trying to tell me something?" Shirley asked and tittered.

He smothered her laughter with his mouth while his hands worked at removing her dress. Exposing her bosom, he applied his tongue to her left nipple. Her back arched, her fingers dug into his shoulders, and her leg rubbed hard against him. He shifted to her right breast, then alternated from one to the other, swirling each nipple and squeezing each globe until she panted with unrestrained desire.

"Keep it up, lover," Shirley coaxed. "Don't ever stop. I'm in heaven."

"You haven't seen anything yet," Fargo said and plunged his right hand under the folds of her dress to get at her innermost treasure. At the insertion of his forefinger, she bucked into the air and bit him on the arm. He worked his finger in and almost out, over and over again, as her moving bottom matched his rhythm. Her lips became hot coals. Her tongue lathered his neck.

He was in no mood to rush. It had been a few weeks since last he shared a woman's bed, and he wanted to savor every passionate second—which might be hard to do. Shirley was tremendously experienced in the art of lovemaking and knew just where to touch and kiss him to drive him to even higher heights of carnal hunger. Exercising self-control became increasingly more difficult.

Hiking her dress around her slim waist, Fargo admired Shirley's flawless thighs. He ran a hand over her glassy skin, listening to her moan and sigh, and felt a lump form in his throat. She was like a lush fruit ripe for the picking, her legs spread wide in invitation.

"Love me, honey," she said. "Please."

Against his better judgment, Fargo eased in an inch or two, then rammed in all the way to the hilt. Squealing and thrashing, she met his thrusts with vigor, giving as good as she got. Here was a woman who reveled in physical pleasure and never held back once her fires were stoked.

Fargo paced himself, stroking at an even tempo while kissing her face and fondling her breasts. The bed creaked and sagged. Gripping her behind, he slammed into her like a steam engine piston, and Shirley matched him.

"Oh!" she suddenly cried, her mouth wide. "I'm coming already! Oh, my! Take me there, lover! Take me!"

So much for not rushing. Fargo exploded with the force of a stick of dynamite. Every square inch of his skin throbbed, and the veins on his neck bulged. He pounded away until he couldn't pound any more, then he sagged on top of her, relishing the sensation of being sexually satisfied. A little rest, he figured, and he would go at it again. Shirley, however, wasn't inclined to wait that long.

"That was wonderful!" she declared, her hands roving below his waist. "Now let's see what it takes to get you up to doing it again."

4

The tantalizing odor of frying bacon and eggs brought Fargo out of a deep, dreamless slumber. Yawning, he sat up in bed and wryly regarded the crumpled sheet, blanket, and quilt. It looked as if a battle had taken place, and in a sense one had. Shirley had kept him going until the wee hours of the morning, her lovemaking violently intense as the bite and scratch marks on his arms and back proved. When at last they'd fallen into an exhausted sleep, she had been nibbling on his inner thighs in an effort to arouse him for a fourth bout. The woman was insatiable.

He slid out of bed and hastily donned his clothes. The toothpick was still where it should be in his boot. As he strapped the gunbelt on, he ambled out into the front room and saw her busy at the stove, humming to herself. "Morning," he said.

"Morning, hell! It's afternoon. You've about slept the day away."

Fargo moved to the window and gazed at the azure sky to find the sun had passed its zenith an hour ago. "I didn't mean to sleep this long," he commented.

"Take a seat and I'll have a heaping plate ready for you in a minute," Shirley said. "I'm a darn good cook, if I do say so myself."

Once at the table he propped his elbows on the top and rested his chin in his hands. Shirley wore a robe that clung to her assets and revealed enough cleavage to tempt a monk. He idly contemplated stripping the robe off and taking her right there on the table, but his growling stomach held him in check.

"Are you open to some advice, handsome?" she unexpectedly asked.

"Depends on what it is."

Shirley stopped what she was doing and faced him, her expression grave. "I want you to promise me that after you're done eating you'll saddle up and ride out of Serenity and never, ever come back."

"I'm not quite ready to leave yet," Fargo told her.

"Listen to me," she said, coming toward him. "Do as I say. Go out the door, turn left, and go behind the house. Stay at the back of the buildings until you get to the livery. Make sure no one sees you."

"Why should I go to all that bother? I'm not afraid of Ringald."

Shirley's lips compressed. "It's not him I'm thinking of." She rested a hand on his wrist. "There is more going on here than you know, and I don't want you ending your days like Charlie Pitman. Please." She squeezed until it hurt. "Please sneak out of town with no one the wiser. You'll regret it if you don't."

"Why?"

"I can't tell you. Just trust me."

"I do. But unless you give me a good reason, I aim to stay until I find the man I'm looking for."

Shirley suddenly whirled and went to the stove. "Damn you," she muttered. "Damn all men and their hard heads!" She flipped the bacon and poked the eggs with a fork.

Now was the time to press her, Fargo figured. After the intimate night they'd shared, she might open up with some prying. "All you have to do is give me a reason," he reiterated. "You must know all there is to know about Serenity. What secret are you hiding?"

She angrily jabbed the eggs but made no reply.

"Charlie Pitman was scared to death of someone, so scared he tried to steal my horse to get away," Fargo said. "He mentioned a man named Cutler. Is that the hombre in the buckskins? Who is he? How does he fit in with Traute and this valley?"

"You ask too many questions."

"What did Pitman get himself into? Did he do something to get on Traute's bad side?"

Taking plates from the cupboard, Shirley loaded his with enough food to feed a grizzly and brought the plate over. As she put it down, he touched her hand.

"Why won't you tell me?"

41

She looked him in the eyes. "You're a fool, Fargo. You think you can help when there is nothing you can do. Vincent Traute has this valley sewn up tight. Give him grief and you'll soon be planted three feet under. Take my word for it. I've seen enough men die because of him."

"Where do I find Cutler? At Traute's ranch?" Fargo prompted, and was surprised to see tears suddenly stream down her cheeks. Scowling, she turned, dashed into the bedroom, and slammed the door.

He could hear her sobbing and the creak of the springs as she threw herself onto the bed. Well, he'd certainly handled that well! Annoyed, he began eating, taking his time, hoping she would come back out. But she didn't. When he was done, he stood and stepped to the bedroom door. "Shirley?"

"Go away!"

"We should talk."

"I have nothing more to say to you. If you want to get yourself killed, then go ahead! I've done all I can." She sniffled, then resumed crying.

Fargo tried the latch but found the door was locked. Rather than waste his breath trying to persuade her to change her mind, he moved to the corner and retrieved his gear. With the saddle in his right hand, the Sharps in his left, the bedroll under his left arm, and his saddlebags slung over his left shoulder, he went out, squinting in the brilliant sunshine.

Serenity was as dead as ever. Anyone who didn't know any better would swear it was a ghost town.

He walked to the saloon, placed his belongings against the wall to the left of the bat-wing doors, then entered. Griswald stood behind the bar cleaning a shot glass. Burke and another of Traute's men sat at a card table. The mongrel dog lay in the corner, snoozing.

"Hello again, stranger," the bartender called. "Care for a drink?"

Fargo placed the Sharps on the bar top, then ordered a whiskey and gulped it down. He glanced in the mirror and happened to notice the man called Burke staring spitefully at his back. In a testy mood anyway because he was no closer to finding the bushwhacker after a whole day in town and because he had so upset Shirley, he gave rein to his anger and spun, resting his elbows on the edge of the bar. "You have a problem, mister," he announced.

"Me?" Burke blurted.

"Yep," Fargo said, stepping to the man's chair and poising his hand near his Colt. "This make's twice I've caught you staring at me like you wished someone would fill me with lead. And I don't like it."

Burke was a stocky man with fleshy features partially offset by a thick mustache and bushy sideburns. He fidgeted, put down his cards, and said lamely. "I don't know who you think you are, mister. There's no law against looking at a man."

Fargo bent down. "It's not the law you have to worry about. It's *me*."

"Now hold on there, you two!" Griswald shouted. "I don't want any trouble in here." He paused. "Don't mind Burke none, stranger. He's just jealous. For months now he's been pining after Shirley, and he can't stand for her to take a man to her place."

"So that's it," Fargo said, unbending. "You must have hated Charlie Pitman, too. Maybe you had a hand in his death."

"I don't know any Pitman," Burke responded without a shred of conviction.

Fargo was positive the man lied. But short of throttling the truth out of the spineless clod, there was little he could do. Letting his disgust show, he stepped to the bar and said, "One more before I hit the trail." He had seen enough of Serenity for the time being. It might be wise, he concluded, to scout around the valley and circle back to the town later. If he hid nearby and kept his eyes peeled, he might just spot the man he was after.

"You're leaving us so soon?" Griswald said with a grin as he poured. "Shirley's charms must not be what they once were."

Fargo gave him a hard stare.

"I'll tally your bill so you can pay up before you ride out," Griswald said quickly. Putting down the bottle, he moved to a doorway leading to a back room. "Won't be a minute," he added, wiping his hands on his apron.

"I'm in no hurry," Fargo said. He sipped the drink slowly, checked in the mirror to see if Burke was still glaring at him and saw the man preoccupied with the card game, then pushed his hat back and reviewed all that had happened since arriving in the town. From the rear of the building he heard the sound of a door opening and closing. He wondered if the bartender had gone out for some reason.

Taking the Sharps, Fargo walked to the long table and sat down facing the front entrance. He mustn't forget that Ringald might be gunning for him. The gunman could show up at any time, so he must stay alert. Polishing off the last of his drink, he set the glass aside and stretched. Somewhere out on the street a horse whinnied. Curious, he was about to rise and take a look when the barkeep hastened through the doorway behind the bar and came toward him waving a sheet of paper.

"Sorry it took so long," Griswald apologized. "I misplaced the darn thing." He halted and offered the paper to Fargo. "Care to see if the list I made is right?"

"I doubt you'd try to cheat me," Fargo said, leaning back and reaching for his pocket. "Just tell me how much it is."

"Fair enough," Griswald responded. He held the paper up and read off the total. "The way I have it figured, you owe four hundred and seventy-five dollars. That doesn't include the town tax."

Fargo glanced up sharply and started to smile, thinking the bartender was joking at his expense. "Oh? And how much is the tally with the tax?"

Griswald looked at the paper, then set it on the table. "Four hundred and eighty-three dollars. I just hope you don't have a lot of big bills. I'm a little short on change right now."

Fargo was waiting for the man to break into laughter, but Griswald appeared dead serious. Fargo picked up the sheet to see the actual total for himself and couldn't believe his eyes. "What the hell is this?" he snapped.

"Did I make a mistake?" Griswald replied. "I don't see how I could. The prices are all listed there." He counted them off on his fingers. "Fifty dollars for a bottle of whiskey. Seventy-five dollars for two meals. Forty dollars livery fee. Ten dollars for the two drinks you just had. And three hundred for room and board."

"Room and board?" Fargo said harshly, rising.

"That's the polite way of putting it," Griswald said. "You did spend the night with Shirley, remember?"

"I'm in no mood for games," Fargo said, throwing the sheet down. "I want to know how much I really owe, and I want to know now."

"Four hundred and eighty-three dollars."

What little patience Fargo had left evaporated. He angrily strode around the table and seized the bartender by the front of the shirt. Griswald, surprisingly, made no effort to resist. "I don't know what you're trying to pull here mister, and I don't much care," Fargo stated gruffly. "Even in a big city like New Orleans I wouldn't have to pay more than fifteen dollars for everything I had. So I'll give you fifteen, and we'll call it square."

"I can't do that, sir. Your total is four hundred and eighty-three dollars."

"Like hell it is," Fargo said. Letting go, he took the small roll of bills he carried and began to peel off fifteen dollars.

"I'm afraid this won't sit well with Mr. Traute," Griswald remarked. "He's the one who sets the prices."

"Then I'll take it up with him."

"You do that," said a voice from the entrance.

Turning, Fargo saw Vincent Traute shove through the bat-wing doors. Today the man wore an expensive gray suit and a matching hat. Marshal Ward and two other men followed, the lawman carrying a shotgun in the crook of his left arm.

"Is there a problem here?" Traute addressed Griswald.

"I'm afraid so, sir. This man refuses to pay his bill. He claims he's being overcharged."

"Give me the bill," Traute demanded, and when the bartender handed it over, he studied the notations for several seconds, then frowned. "What is the meaning of this, Mr. Griswald?"

"Sir?"

"Our guest is right. You did make a mistake." Traute gave the sheet to the barkeep. "I happen to know that Shirley fed him earlier, so you need to add another twenty dollars. The grand total should be five hundred and three dollars, including the tax." He faced Fargo. "I'm truly sorry about the mix-up."

For a fleeting moment Fargo had thought that Traute was going to set matters straight. Now he realized otherwise, and he also saw that the marshal and the two men had fanned out so that each of them had a clear shot if necessary. Over at the card table Burke and his partner had risen and were standing with their hands near their holsters. He was hemmed in. It didn't take a great genius to figure out that he had blundered into a crooked setup of some kind, and with a sinking feeling he knew he must be extremely careful.

"Now then," Traute said to him. "How would you like to pay? Cash, gold, or silver are all acceptable."

"I'll ask you the same thing I asked Griswald," Fargo said, struggling to keep his tone level. "What the hell are you trying to pull? I don't have that kind of money and you know it."

"You don't?" Traute said, acting astonished. "This is quite a shock. Why did you order all that food and drink, not to mention availing yourself of Shirley's services, if you didn't have the money to pay for everything?"

"In any other town I wouldn't have to pay more than ten or fifteen dollars."

"Ah, yes. But you're in Serenity, and Serenity is my town. I charge for goods and services as I please. You really should have asked about the prices before you went on your spending spree." Traute made a clucking sound. "And now you have the gall to tell us you don't have enough money to cover your bill? Here I thought you were a man of honor."

Fargo balled his right fist and went to take a step when the crisp click of a gun hammer being drawn back drew his gaze to Ward. The marshal had leveled and cocked the shotgun. One move and he would be blown in half.

"What *are* we going to do?" Traute said. "I can't just let you ride off without paying. We'll have to come to some sort of accommodation." He rubbed his palms together. "How much money do you have on you?"

So that was their game, Fargo decided. Traute would demand every cent he owned as payment, and they would send him packing. "I have about forty dollars," he answered.

"Is that all?" Traute asked and sighed. "That's not much, but it will do for a start."

"A start?" Fargo said and wondered if they might try to take the Ovaro and his personal effects to make up the difference. Over his dead body, he silently vowed.

"Yes. I'm afraid you must pay the full bill before you can be allowed to leave Serenity," Traute said. "Since you don't have enough money, I have an idea that might satisfy both of us."

"I can hardly wait to hear it," Fargo said dryly.

"Your sarcasm, sir, is uncalled for. I have only your best interests at heart. If you refuse to make good on your account, that's the same as stealing. Marshal Ward will have to jail you until your trial, and I can guarantee the judge does not think highly of cheats and thieves."

"Let me guess," Fargo said. "You're the judge."

Traute grinned. "How did you know? Yes, as a matter of fact, I am. As such, I would be compelled to give you a lengthy sentence in our jail, which, sad to say, leaves a lot to be desired where comfort and cleanliness are concerned." He stopped, his grin widening. "Or you can earn the difference due by working for me."

Fargo cocked his head, studying the phony bastard. Here was an unexpected angle. "What kind of work?" he asked.

"You'll receive three meals a day, and your living quarters will be no worse than the jail would be."

"What kind of work?" Fargo stressed.

"I think I should save that as a surprise," Traute said. "What do you say? Do we have an agreement?"

Fargo held his arms loose at his sides, squared his shoulders, and answered, "Mister, I wouldn't agree to giving you the time of day. You're as low-down as they come. Ringald might be a sidewinder, but he's a saint compared to you."

"Should I take that as a no?"

"Take it any way you like."

"What a pity," Traute said. "I had hoped we could conduct this like civilized men." Stepping swiftly backward, he nodded at the lawman.

Marshal Ward advanced a step, the shotgun steady in his hands. "All right, stranger. Mr. Traute has tried his best to be reasonable, but you don't leave him no choice. I want you to unfasten your gunbelt, then let your six-gun fall to the floor." He lifted the barrel until it pointed at Fargo's head. "And I don't think I need to spell out what will happen if you try anything fancy."

Fargo barely held back his rage. Suddenly, at a signal from Traute, the other men in the room all drew their revolvers. Should Fargo so much as twitch the wrong way, a hail of lead would drop him where he stood.

"We're waiting," Ward said.

"Please be sensible," Traute chimed in. "I have no wish to harm you. Despite what you might think, I'm a man of my word. You'll have your bill paid off in no time and be on your way."

Now Fargo knew how a cornered mountain lion felt. He wanted to lash out, to rip Traute apart and blast the others into eternity, but there was absolutely nothing he could do. His sense of burning frustration was limitless. Moving slowly, he undid his buckle and listened to the thud as the gunbelt landed near his boots.

"I knew you would come around to my way of thinking," Traute boasted. He nodded at one of the men, who stepped in close to Fargo and picked up the gunbelt. Traute visibly relaxed, as did Marshal Ward and the others. Ward lowered the shotgun and the others let their revolvers droop slightly. The man holding the gunbelt turned to move to one side.

Fargo struck with the speed of a cottonmouth. He shoved the one with his gun and sent the man crashing into the lawman. Then, before any of the rest could aim and fire, he leaped, his hands encircling Traute's neck, the force of his lunge bearing them both to the floor. Shouts erupted as he twisted and rolled to the left, bearing the startled Traute with him.

"Don't shoot, you fools!" Marshal Ward bellowed. "You might hit Mr. Traute!"

In two rolls Fargo was at the bat-wing doors. Traute came out of his daze and clawed ineffectually at Fargo's wrists. A knee to the groin put an end to that. Footsteps pounded, closing from all directions. Releasing Traute, Fargo rolled once more under the bat-wing doors and into the street. He leaped up and saw three horses at the hitching post but realized Traute's men would be on him before he could untie one of the animals, mount, and race off. Already an enraged face had appeared in the doorway.

Whirling, Fargo sped toward the barn. He was a fast runner, and if he could gain a dozen yards on his pursuers, he'd be able to effect his escape. No one could catch him once he was on the Ovaro. The barn doors were wide open, making his task easier.

A glance back showed Ward, Burke, and three other men spilling from the saloon. They pounded after him, swirls of dust rising from under their boots. He also spied Shirley and another woman, undoubtedly her friend Gloria, standing in front of their house, their mouths agape.

"Stop, damn you!" Marshal Ward yelled. "You can't get away!"

Who was the lawman trying to kid? Fargo reflected, exerting himself to the limit. He was ten yards ahead of them and gaining with each long stride. At the livery he bolted inside, dashed to the stall containing the Ovaro, and pulled the stallion out. Since there was no time to saddle up, his saddle and blanket would have to hang where they were until he came back—which he would, once he got his hands on a rifle and revolver. He was going to make Traute pay with a vengeance.

Gripping the stallion's mane, he swung up. Ward and the others were close, judging by their drumming footsteps, but they had slowed, perhaps guessing his intent and wary of being run down as he galloped out the front. Let them keep thinking that, he reflected, smirking, and wheeled the Ovaro. At the back was a smaller door still large enough to get through if he bent forward over the Ovaro's neck. A jab of his heels took him there. He had to stop long enough to lean down and throw the door wide. Then, ducking low, he eased the pinto into the opening.

The Ovaro's head cleared the jambs. Sunlight hit his face and he started to straighten. He heard a hiss of air a moment before something rammed into his left temple. Stars exploded before his eyes and he sagged, his mind reeling. Another blow connected, this time knocking him off the pinto. He was vaguely aware of crashing onto his side. The world spun wildly, his stomach churned, and a dim haze enveloped him. He thought he saw the face of the piano player, the one responsible for tending the livery, Jeeter, and thought he heard Jeeter speak.

"Sorry, mister. But this will earn me an extra bottle or two, I reckon."

5

Fargo first heard a peculiar muted clanking, as if a black-smith was striking an anvil with a hammer a great distance off. As his senses sharpened, he realized the clanking was much closer at hand. He also inhaled a dank odor, like freshly dug earth. There was a dull ache in his head, but otherwise he felt fine.

Fargo opened his eyes and took stock. He was lying on his back, his hands folded on his chest. Eight feet above him was a ceiling of unpainted wooden planks. Glancing to his right, he found a plank wall. To his left was a ten-foot square room with an earthen floor. In the center sat a rickety table and four chairs. Ringing the room along the walls were a half-dozen dilapidated beds.

"Well, look who's finally awake. I reckon we'll have us some help tomorrow, boys."

Rising on an elbow, Fargo studied the four men before him. Two were seated on beds, two were at the table, playing cards using an dog-eared deck. All of them wore grimy, tattered clothes, and all had unkempt beards and hair. Their dirty faces were unnaturally pale, and their bodies lean from lack of proper food. "Who are you?" he asked. "Where am I?"

The man who had spoken first, a wizened old-timer whose face was as craggy as a mountain cliff and who was one of the men playing cards, snorted and said, "Now where have I heard those questions before?" He looked at Fargo. "You're in hell, son, and here you'll likely stay until the devil done buries you."

Fargo sat up and swung his legs over the side of the low bed. As he did, he heard a clinking noise and something tugged at his left ankle. Glancing down, he was stunned to see a large iron ball and a three-foot length of chain had been attached to his leg while he was unconscious. "What the hell!" he blurted and leaned down to tug at the chain, which was attached to his ankle by a tight metal shackle.

"Ain't it a beauty?" asked the man at the table. "You'll get used to it, son. Trust me. We all went through the same thing."

Only then did Fargo see that all four men wore similar balls and chains. "Traute!" he growled and wrenched on the chain with all his strength. The shackle didn't budge.

"You're wastin' your breath, son."

Fargo paid no heed. He wedged his fingers under the shackle and tried prying the metal outward, to no avail. He gripped the links nearest the shackle and pulled until his face became bright red and his neck muscles stood out like cords of rope, yet accomplished nothing. Furious, he stood and lifted the heavy ball. "Where's Traute?" he demanded. "I want to see him."

"You'll have to wait until morning. He won't come out to the mine until then, son."

"Quit calling me your damn son," Fargo snapped and picked up the heavy ball in both hands. The metal was smooth and cool to the touch. Holding it just below his waist, he moved toward a closed door in one corner, shuffling awkwardly because of the chain and ignoring the amused stares of the four men.

"Don't do anything stupid, mister," said a big-boned man on one of the beds.

"Yeah," chimed in a man whose Adam's apple was as big as an orange. "You'll regret it if you do. They get right riled when one of us makes trouble."

"I'm not sitting still for this," Fargo said. He reached the corner, dropped the ball, and pounded on the door with both fists. The door shook under his blows, threatening to break off its hinges. Suddenly sharp cries broke out on the other side. Seconds later the door was thrown open, and a huge bear of a man, dressed in a flannel shirt and jeans and carrying a stout club, filled the doorway.

"What the hell do you think you're doing?" he demanded.

"I want to see Traute," Fargo shot back. "Fetch him. Now."

The man's eyes were ablaze with simmering resentment. He hefted the club, scowled, and replied, "You're giving *me* orders are you?"

Another man appeared behind the irate giant. He also toted a club. "What's wrong, Creel? What's all the ruckus about?"

"The new man is acting up, Rufus, just like Mr. Traute said he would," Creel answered. "He thinks he can boss us around."

"Show him how wrong he is," Rufus said.

Fargo saw the swing coming and glided backward to avoid it. Or tried to, until his left boot became caught on the chain, throwing him off balance. Frantically he tried to regain his footing, and for a moment he neglected to keep an eye on Creel. The club caught him full in the stomach, and doubled him over in agony, the breath whooshing from his lungs. Sputtering and coughing, he attempted to straighten but received a resounding crack on the head. His legs weakened, and his knees buckled.

"Get this straight, mister," Creel declared, towering over him. "*I* give the orders here, not you. If you don't do what I say when I say it, you'll get more of this." His boot flicked out, searing Skye's ribs.

"Please, Creel!" called out the wizened card player. "Don't be so hard on him. He's just arrived. He doesn't know all the rules yet."

"Keep out of this, Haggerty," the giant hissed, "or you'll get some of the same treatment." With a contemptuous shove of the club, he knocked Fargo to the floor. "You'd better learn the rules, mister, and learn them fast. If you act up again, I'm liable to stomp you into the dirt."

Fargo heard the door slam shut. His head on the floor, he inhaled deeply and struggled to suppress the pain.

"We tried to warn you, friend," someone said.

A hand fell lightly on Fargo's shoulder, and he twisted to see the man called Haggerty.

"None of us blames you," Haggerty said. "It's quite a shock to wake up and find yourself wearin' one of these." He gave the shackle around his ankle a smack. "We've all been through what you're feelin'."

The man with the prominent Adam's apple came over, and Fargo let himself be helped to a chair. His stomach

53

felt queasy, and his head throbbed. "Where are we?" he asked.

"In a cabin near the mine," Haggerty answered. "Before I give you the low-down, I should let you meet the rest." He pointed at the other card player, a young man with long brown hair who had not uttered a word since Fargo came around. "This here is Carson. He's not the friendliest galoot you'll ever meet, but he holds his own when there's work to do."

"Howdy," Carson said.

Pivoting, Haggerty indicated the big-boned man. "That's Rice. He's as strong as an ox, which comes in handy when we have to haul beams and such."

"Pleased to meet you," Rice said.

Finally Haggerty turned to the man with the oversized Adam's apple. "And this is Yost. He's been here pretty near as long as I have. You'd think the mine would have claimed us by now, but we're both stubborn cusses. And we're both right fond of livin'."

"What mine is this you keep mentioning?"

"Why, Traute's silver mine, what else?" Haggerty said. "Or didn't he tell you about his secret?"

"No."

"Then let me do the honors," Haggerty said, taking a seat. "Once you understand what's going on, you won't give Traute's men an excuse to beat up on you. Not if you want to stay healthy." He rested his forearms on the tabletop and leaned forward. "First off, what do you know about the wonderful town of Serenity?"

"Not much. I had no idea there was a town in these parts until I stumbled on it."

"Few do know Serenity exists," Haggerty said. "It got its start as an outlaw den back in 1849. South of here, you see, is an old trail that pilgrims from the States followed on their way to California during the big gold rush. Some of those pilgrims struck it rich and headed back to their loved ones by the same way. And a lot of them never made it home."

"Must we suffer through this old tale of yours again?" Carson interrupted. "I'd much rather play cards."

"In a bit," Haggerty told him and went on. "It was a skunk by the name of Haskill who first found the valley and took to hidin' out here between attacks on the gold seekers headin' back from California. Traute joined the gang later. For a while they had a real good thing goin', then the rush panned out and there was no one to rob." He coughed. "Long about that time, one of the men out huntin' found a promisin' silver vein on a mountain at the west end of the valley. The outlaws took to squabblin' among themselves over how to dig the silver out and how big their shares should be. Traute won the argument by killin' Haskill and the man who found the vein."

"What happened next?" Fargo prompted when Haggerty stopped to scratch his armpit.

"Traute was made the new leader. He had the brainstorm to set up their own little town. Not that they cared all that much for the creature comforts. Traute, you see, had figured out a way of gettin' the men they needed to do the diggin'."

Fargo could see it all in his mind's eye. It would be just like a band of shiftless outlaws, men too downright lazy or plain unwilling to earn their wages honestly, to resort to forcing others to perform the hard labor.

"Every so often some poor soul would wander into Serenity or be tricked into comin' here by members of the gang who took a lot of trips to the settlements after goods and supplies. And once they lured someone in, they'd rig up charges and put the man to work in their mine. Simple as that."

"So that explains everything," Fargo said.

"Traute is a rotten son of a bitch, but he's a crafty, rotten son of a bitch," Haggerty declared. "He knew it would take years to get all the silver out, and that he couldn't expect to keep his men happy if they were all stuck in a little cabin. But a whole town all to themselves is another story."

"Traute is smart in more ways than that," Yost interjected. "He always has the last word on men they pick to work in the mine, and he always picks men no one will miss. Drifters, saddle tramps, or men with no kin, like Rice there."

"Yes, sir," Haggerty said. "Traute has thought of everything. If I didn't hate the miserable polecat so much, I'd almost admire him."

Full comprehension only fueled Fargo's anger, some of which was directed at himself. He had fallen for

Traute's trap with his eyes wide open. Shirley must have known what was going to happen, which was why she had wanted him to ride out of town without letting anyone know. She'd tried to warn him, but he hadn't listened.

"Yes, sir," Haggerty said. "A lot of good men have come and gone since I was put to work." His face clouded. "A lot of good men have died."

"How many have escaped?" Fargo inquired.

Every man there brightened.

"Just one, and that was a few days ago," Haggerty responded, lowering his voice and casting an anxious glance at the door. "His name is Charlie Pitman, and once he gets back to Fort Leavenworth, he'll inform the army of what's been going on and this nest of vipers will be cleaned out. We'll be free at last."

"At last!" Yost echoed.

All the pieces of the puzzle now fit. Fargo understood why Pitman had been desperate enough to try and steal his horse. And it was obvious that it had been one of Traute's men who had hunted Pitman down. Adding insult to injury, the killer must have deliberately led Fargo back to Serenity, perhaps planning all along to have him wind up in the mine. Traute wouldn't want any witnesses to Pitman's murder.

"I can't wait for the army to get here!" Haggerty said excitedly. "I'll be the first one to testify at Traute's trial. I want to see him hanged so bad I can taste it!"

"And I still say you're getting your hopes up for nothing, old man," Carson said. "The army doesn't have much jurisdiction in civilian matters. And don't forget that Traute has arranged everything nice and legal. He'll give the army proof we all broke laws and claim that we all had fair trials and were found guilty. What can the army do in a case like that?"

"Maybe not much," Rice said doubtfully.

"Don't listen to this young dunderhead," Haggerty chided. "Pitman will have us rescued. You wait and see."

"If he's smart, he'll keep on going and not tell a soul," Carson remarked.

Haggerty puffed up his chest and glowered. "Charlie would never do a yellow-bellied thing like that! He's a man to ride the river with, and I should know since he was better friends with me than he was with you. He'll save us."

In the expectant silence that followed, Fargo's voice was like the peal of doom. "No, he won't."

"What's that?" Haggerty asked, facing him. "What did you say?"

"Charlie Pitman is dead, bushwhacked by a man in buckskins and a fur hat. I was there. I saw him die."

All the men swore vehemently. Haggerty, incensed, pounded the table, then sagged in his chair and groaned in despair. Carson, the one who had been the most skeptical, was the most affected; his face contorted in anguish, he closed his eyes and sorrowfully bowed his head.

"You say you were there?" Yost asked. "How did it happen?"

Fargo told them. He disliked being the bearer of such bad news, so he kept the story brief. They were four broken men when he finished, their spirits crushed, their hopes dashed. "I'm sorry," he concluded. "I wish Pitman had told me right off what was wrong, but he didn't."

"He probably didn't know if he could trust you or not," Haggerty said. "Maybe he figured you might be workin' for Traute."

"I rode into Serenity after the man who killed him," Fargo disclosed, surveying the room. "I never counted on something like this."

"The man you want is Jeff Cutler," Yost said. "He's been working for Traute for about six months now, and they say he can track an ant over solid rock."

Jeffery Cutler! The name jarred Fargo's memory like a lightening bolt. Now he knew why they had been so evenly matched during their fight in the forest. Now he knew why the sight of the moccasin print had stirred his recollection. Cutler had long been a familiar name to those who lived in the Rockies. Trapper, mountain man, scout, guide—Cutler had done it all. According to the tale tellers, Cutler had once taken an Arapaho wife and been adopted into their tribe. Not long ago, Blackfeet had slain her and their children. Now Cutler roamed the wild mountains like a rabid wolf, friendly to no man, red or white. How had he come to work for Traute? Fargo wondered.

"I reckon this changes everything," Haggerty commented forlornly. "It looks as if I'll end my days down in that dark hole after all."

"Not if I can help it," Fargo said.

Carson ran his hand through his long hair. "Big words from someone who has no idea what he's up against. It was a miracle that Charlie escaped. The rest of us will never have the same chance. They watch us too closely now."

"How did Pitman do it?"

"He got his hands on a short piece of wire and kept fiddling with the lock on his shackle. Must have worked at it for three months off and on, whenever he could without them catching him, but it wouldn't open," Carson said. "Then one day, when he was helping Rice with the ore carts, Rufus let them take a short breather up on top. Charlie started in on the lock, and damn if it didn't pop open. Rufus wasn't paying too much attention to them, and Charlie lit out like a jackrabbit. By the time Rufus and Creel got word to Traute, Charlie was long gone."

"Now they always watch us like hawks when we take breathers," Yost mentioned. "Traute has made it plain that they'll pay with their lives if one of us gets away again."

"Are Creel and Rufus the only guards?" Fargo asked.

"Yep," Carson said. "That's all they need. One of them is always down in the hole with us while the other stands watch at the mine entrance."

Fargo pondered the information. If he could get close enough to either of the guards, he'd have all of them free in no time. He could feel the slender sheath to his Arkansas toothpick rubbing against his ankle, and he smiled at how careless Traute's men had been. Leaning down, he slipped his fingers into his boot and groped for the hilt of the throwing knife. But just the sheath was there. The knife was gone!

Haggerty noticed what he was doing and said, "It ain't there, son. I saw Creel and Rufus search you when Marshal Ward brought you in. They found your knife."

"Damn," Fargo fumed.

"Creel is a heartless jackass, but he's not as dumb as he looks," Haggerty said. "There's not much he misses."

"And he likes to hurt people," Carson said. "Give him

an excuse—any excuse, no matter how small—and he'll beat you black and blue. You got off easy tonight, believe me."

"And Rufus?"

"He's Creel's shadow. He's not quite the brute Creel is, but he has his moments. And Rufus is fast with his hands. Keep that in mind if you ever get any crazy notions."

"I will," Fargo said. There was much more he wanted to learn about the mining operation, but before he could voice his questions, the door was hurled wide and in strode the brutal giant, Creel.

"Time for you to get your rest, gents. We want you up to snuff tomorrow."

The four captives dutifully stepped to their beds, each man picking up the iron ball to which he was attached. Fargo shuffled toward his bed but dragged the ball behind him. Without warning, a hard blow to his lower back propelled him forward to sprawl over the bed, his body racked by pain. Twisting, he stared up into Creel's cruel face.

"You don't know all the rules yet, so I didn't break your spine," the brutal guard said with a sneer. "From now on, you'll carry your ball when you go anywhere. If you don't, you'll regret it. Savvy?"

Fargo was seeing red. He clenched his teeth, tempted to smash a fist into Creel's mouth.

"I asked you something, mister," the giant said, hefting his club. "Answer me, or so help me I'll bust your nose as flat as a pancake. The boss says we have to keep all of you alive, but he also says we can break a few bones if you won't behave."

As much as it galled Fargo to be bullied and manhandled, he knew he must swallow his pride or be severely beaten. "I understand," he said crisply.

"Good." Creel moved to the lantern hanging from a long peg on the wall near the door. "Another rule, mister, is that there is no talking once the light goes out. We check now and then, and if we hear so much as a peep out of any of you, all of you pay the price." He picked up the lantern and lifted the globe to blow out the flame, his beady eyes lingering on Fargo. "Savvy?"

"Yes," Fargo said. The room was plunged into darkness, except for the pale light streaming through the doorway. Then the door slammed shut. He could see nothing, not even his hand in front of his face. Lying on his back, he folded his arms and pondered.

There was no way in hell he would stay a prisoner for as long as the other men had been held. The mere thought of being so helpless, of being cooped up in the cabin at night and in the depths of the mine by day, made his skin crawl. To him freedom was everything. Without it a man might as well curl up and die. He loved to roam where he pleased, to constantly explore the wonders of the untamed country stretching between the Mississippi and the Pacific, the Ovaro under him, never knowing what awaited him around the next bend in the trail.

Suddenly loud rumbling broke out on his left, and Fargo realized that one of the men had already fallen asleep. He knew their labors in the mine must leave them exhausted by the end of each day, and he was troubled because by tomorrow night he would be equally tired.

Somehow he must escape soon. If he failed, or if he waited too long, his strength would ebb, his resolve would weaken, just as with the others. Haggerty and the rest were prime examples of what happened to men when they weakened and lost their will to fight for what was right. And it wasn't going to happen to him!

He had no weapons. He had no friends he could count on for help. He was outnumbered and shackled. But one way or the other he was going to get loose and bring Traute's little empire crashing down. Traute was the key, the one with the brains. Without him the rest of the gang would scatter to the four winds.

How long he lay there, thinking, he couldn't say. Everyone in the cabin was snoring when his eyes finally fluttered shut and his battered body relaxed enough for him to start to drift off to sleep. So much had happened since he encountered Charlie Pitman that it was almost like a dream. He tried telling himself that he would awaken in the morning to find himself beside a cold mountain stream, the stallion his sole companion, the incidents of the past couple of days nothing but the work of his vivid imagination.

But he knew better.

6

"Get up, you lazy drifter!"

The gravelly bellow jarred Fargo awake a second before a heavy object gouged into his stomach. He sat up with a start, pain coursing through him, and found Creel towering above the bed.

"On your feet! Someone is here to see you!"

Fargo slowly rose. Across the room Rufus was rousing Haggerty and Carson. He remembered to pick up the heavy ball and took a step. Creel, fidgeting impatiently, gave him a rough shove toward the doorway.

"Faster. We can't keep the boss waiting."

Outside the air was fresh and cool. Dawn touched the eastern horizon with streaks of pink and yellow, while a few white clouds sailed overhead and birds sang everywhere.

Fargo saw a small group of horsemen to his left, beside an ominous opening at the base of a short cliff. The cabin, he discovered, sat to the south of the mine. To the east and north was a forested slope running down to the valley floor. Serenity was visible down below, smoke curling upward from several buildings.

Vincent Traute, smiling enigmatically, sat on a fine roan, Ringald to his right. To his left were Ward, Burke, and another man, a man Fargo had never met but whom he knew at first sight, a wiry figure dressed in buckskins and a beaver hat, the notorious mountain man Jeff Cutler.

"I trust you slept well?" Traute said dryly.

"Never better," Fargo replied.

"I won't keep you long since I know how eager you must be to start to work," Traute said. "But I want you to know exactly where you stand and what will happen to you if you try to buck me."

"You'll have me killed."

"Only if you leave me no choice. But I'm sure Mr. Creel will be able to keep you in line. He's never failed me yet in that regard." Traute rested his hands on the saddle horn. "You've been charged with attempted murder, found guilty, and sentenced to ten years at hard labor. If you try to escape, the deputies will be well within their rights to shoot you dead."

"Creel and Rufus are deputies?"

"Duly sworn in by Marshal Ward himself."

Fargo laughed.

"You won't think this is so funny a week from now when you wake up to the fact you are going to be here for a long, long time. You made the mistake of your life when you attacked me. No man lays a hand on me."

"Climb down from that roan and I'll do it again," Fargo said and was promptly slugged between the shoulder blades by Creel. He staggered but stayed upright, defiantly glaring at his tormentor.

"I can see you have a lot to learn. Well, Mr. Creel will teach you the rules. Learn them well or suffer. It's up to you."

Cutler had been studying Fargo the whole time, a vaguely troubled expression creasing his tanned face. Now he glanced at Traute and asked, "What's the name of this one?"

"What difference does it make?" Traute rejoined.

"There's something about him. I can't quite peg what it is, but I feel I should know him from somewhere."

"Shirley told me his name is Fargo."

The mountain man reacted as if slapped in the face. "Fargo!" he exclaimed. "What's his first name?"

"I never asked. Why?"

Touching the heels of his moccasins to his bay, Jeff Cutler rode up to Fargo and inspected him from head to toe. "Damn you for a fool, Traute. I know you're from Illinois, but you should keep up on things. Don't you know who this man is?"

"He's a nobody, a drifter, a saddle bum like so many others," Traute said, sounding puzzled. "I don't see why he interests you so much."

"Ask him his first name," Cutler said.

"Why should . . ." Traute began, then sighed and

moved up alongside the mountain man. "Very well. What's your first name, Fargo?"

Fargo was the focus of intent interest from every man there. He let a full ten seconds go by before he answered, drawing out the suspense, aware the delay was upsetting Traute. Then he told them.

Ringald, oddly, smiled.

Jeff Cutler slapped a hand on his thigh and declared, "I knew it! Only someone as good as you could have held his own against me the other day." He frowned. "I should have figured it out sooner. If I had, I never would have led you to Serenity."

"I still don't see why you are bothered by this man," Traute said.

With the air of an adult explaining something important to a five-year-old, Cutler said, "This here is Skye Fargo. The Trailsman, they call him. He's one of the best at what he does, and what he does is take tinhorns like you and use them for target practice."

"Have a care, Mr. Cutler," Traute said. "I won't stand for being insulted, not even by you. I pay you good money, and I expect you to treat me with the respect I deserve."

"I always do."

The undercurrent of tension between the two could be cut with a knife. Fargo could see that Cutler didn't much care for Traute, and he made a mental note for future consideration. "There's something I don't understand," he said, looking at Cutler. "What's a man like you doing working for a rabid dog like Traute?"

"Watch your tongue," Creel snarled and swung his club.

This time Fargo was not caught flat-footed. He saw the club descending and whirled, stepping in under the blow to ram his right knee into Creel's groin. His movements were slowed because of the heavy ball and chain but still quick enough to beat the so-called deputy at his own game. The giant tottered backward, his cheeks scarlet, and tensed for another try.

"Enough!" Traute barked.

On his own accord Ringald streaked both pearl-handled pistols from their holsters and leveled them at Fargo. Grinning cockily, he thumbed back both hammers and said, "Give me the word, boss, and this hombre will be pushin' up clover."

"That won't be necessary," Traute said. "Mr. Fargo is no threat to us, despite what Cutler would have me believe. We'll leave Fargo in Creel's capable hands."

"You're making a mistake," Cutler said. "Fargo isn't the kind of man you can take lightly."

"I never take anyone lightly," Traute responded and faced Creel. "Carry on. I expect you to stay on top of things. And I'll be back tomorrow to hear how our new prisoner is doing."

"Don't worry, boss," Creel said. "This bastard won't give us any trouble."

Nodding curtly, Traute gave a wave of his hand, and his band of cutthroats rode down the slope toward Serenity. They were soon lost in the pines.

Fargo would have given anything for a loaded rifle. Rage boiled within him at being treated with such contempt, and it was all he could do to control the anger. Turning, he saw Rufus and the prisoners standing outside the cabin. For the first time he also saw a small shack adjacent to the cabin. That must be where the two guards slept, he figured. Were there guns inside?

The two guards were armed with revolvers carried in military-style holsters sporting leather flaps. A prudent move, since a prisoner who wanted to grab one of the revolvers first had to lift the flap, giving the guard extra time to react.

"All right, you vermin," Rufus said. "If you want your breakfast, line up as usual."

The prisoners formed a row in front of the cabin. Fargo walked over to the end of the line behind Haggerty. He noticed that the ground for thirty feet around both buildings had been cleared of all trees and brush. Anyone foolish enough to make a mad dash from the cabin to the forest must first cross the open space, giving the guards plenty of time to fire. Traute, it seemed, hadn't missed a trick.

While Creel stood guard, Rufus went into the shack and emerged a minute later with a large tin pan of hardtack and a canteen slung over his shoulder.

"Eat hearty, boys," Creel said.

Fargo held up the hard, saltless biscuit he was given and remarked, "Is this all we get?"

"No talking from now on unless you first get permission," Rufus told him. "And yes, that's all you get. Don't complain. It's good hardtack. Griswald makes it. He once served as a cook on a ship."

After the men finished eating, the canteen was passed around. Fargo drank last, and he had taken only three gulps when Creel roughly snatched the canteen away from his grasp.

"That's enough for you, Mr. High-and-Mighty Trailsman. A tough man like you doesn't need that much water."

Rufus put the pan and the canteen back in the shack. Then the prisoners were ordered to move toward the mouth of the mine. In the bright light of the rising sun, Fargo made a number of new discoveries. An ore cart sat just inside the entrance. Stacked against the right-hand wall were a dozen picks and shovels, and nearby lay a pile of coiled rope. Well past the entrance, close to the edge of the trees, was a huge mound of rock and dirt.

"Rice and Carson will handle the cart today," Rufus announced. "The rest of you will be digging." He glanced at Haggerty. "I'm counting on you to teach the new man what to do. If he gives us problems, you suffer, too."

"Does this mean I can talk to him without gettin' in trouble?" Haggerty asked.

"How else are you going to teach him, you old coot?" Rufus responded.

Several shovels and picks were loaded into the cart. While that was taking place, Creel lit three lanterns and gave one to Yost, one to Haggerty, and one to Rice. The giant stayed behind when they began their descent. Rufus brought up the rear, cautiously staying well back so none of them dared jump him.

Fargo felt uneasy from the moment he stepped foot in the shaft. The murky conditions didn't bother him nearly so much as the feeling of being hemmed in, of being confined in an earthen tomb. The ceiling was only seven feet high, the tunnel width less than six feet. Periodically they came upon supporting timbers that had been used to shore the tunnel up. Otherwise they saw nothing but dirt above and below, to the right and the left. A gradual incline took them ever deeper, their shadows playing over the walls like ebony ghosts. Further aggravating him was the constant squeaking of the ore cart's metal wheels. No one had bothered to grease them in ages.

"The tunnel pretty much follows the vein," Haggerty explained. "It goes down about ninety feet, which doesn't sound like much until you think about all the tons of earth over our heads. Whatever you do, don't make any loud noises if you can help it. Always talk in a low voice."

"Has there ever been a cave-in?"

"Not since I was brought here," Haggerty said. "But six months before I rode into Serenity, there was a big cave-in and all of the men down here died. Traute was fit to be tied. It delayed the diggin' until he could get new men to take their place."

"Where is all the ore? I didn't see any up on top."

"A wagon comes two or three times a week and hauls it off to Traute's place. It came yesterday, in fact. You couldn't have seen the wagon trail because it comes up the south side of the mountain to near the cabin, and most of the way the trail is hidden by the trees."

The shaft angled to the right, past a fork now filled from bottom to top with solid earth.

"That's where the cave-in happened," Haggerty said and shuddered. "Thank God I wasn't caught in it. What a horrible way to meet your Maker."

Fargo had to agree. Next to drowning, being smothered to death by inhaling mouthfuls of dirt had to be one of the grisliest deaths imaginable. He stared at the ceiling, his skin prickling as if from a rash, and hoped he wouldn't suffer such a fate.

"I keep tryin' to talk Traute into lettin' us bring birds down, but so far he won't go for it," Haggerty commented.

"Birds?"

"It's an old miner's trick. Sometimes a mining operation will run into a pocket of gas, and before anyone knows what is happening, every man is dead," Haggerty said. "You can't smell the damn stuff, you can't taste it, you don't even know you're breathin' it until it's too late. That is, unless you have a bird. Birds keel over at the first whiff of gas, so when a miner sees *that*, he knows to cut out for the surface pronto."

"You seem to know a lot about mining."

"I've done a little prospecting in my time."

"That's enough, you two!" Rufus abruptly snapped. "Haggerty, I said you could teach Fargo how to do his job. I didn't say you could pass the time of day as you damn well please."

"Sorry, sir," Haggerty said.

Fargo wished the shaft would widen out, but he was disappointed to find it actually narrowed slightly the farther they went, until near the bottom there was barely room for the ore cart to pass through the passageway. Quite unexpectedly they came to the end of the tunnel, a circular area where the walls were lined with glittering ore, and chunks of rock dotted the floor.

"This is it," Haggerty said, taking a pick from the cart and handing another to Fargo. "Our work is pretty simple. Keep chippin' at the rock until you break it off. If it has silver, Rice and Carson will dump it in the cart and take the load up to Creel."

The air, Fargo realized, was muggy and hard to breathe. He inhaled deeply to compensate and felt lightheaded.

"I should have warned you," Haggerty said. "Breathin' takes some gettin' used to this far down. If you get dizzy, just lean on the wall until the spell passes. If you pass out, try to watch where you fall so you don't hit your head on any of the rocks."

"Just don't make a habit of taking a break," Rufus declared. "We don't abide slackers."

Fargo glanced at the guard, who stood ten feet away at the fringe of the flickering lantern light. Rushing him would be suicide. Or would it? Surely neither of the guards would dare fire their weapons so far down and risk causing a cave-in. It was food for thought.

"Get to work!" Rufus commanded.

Lifting the heavy pick, Fargo moved to a section of wall a few feet away and set to work, swinging loosely and easily, the pointed end of the head biting into the ore and sending chips flying. It took no time at all to break into a sweat. He breathed carefully, pacing himself, feeling the strain in his shoulders and wrists.

Soon the shaft echoed to the blows of the picks and the scraping sounds of shovels. Rice and Carson were kept busy inspecting the ore and filling the cart. Rufus leaned against the wall in the background, a coiled rattler ready to strike should any of them get out of line.

Fargo tired much sooner than he would have expected. His lungs ached when he stopped to take a short rest and lowered the pick to the floor to give his sore arms some relief. He had to concentrate with all his might to simply think.

"How are you holdin' up?" Haggerty inquired.

"I feel like I've run five miles under a blistering sun."

"That's normal. Your body will adjust after a while."

"If I live that long."

Hour after strenuous hour went by. Fargo lost all track of time. Eventually they were permitted to take a rest, and he promptly sagged to the floor and sucked in air. They were allowed a single swallow of water. Then it was back to work.

Later they were marched to the surface and given bowls of soup and a single slice of bread apiece. The cool mountain air was like a refreshing spring shower when it struck Fargo's perspiring face, instantly revitalizing him. He dreaded the prospect of venturing below again. To a man who had spent nearly all of his time outdoors, the mine shaft was a living hell. But under the hawkish stares of the two guards, he had no choice but to comply.

The afternoon dragged, grueling minute after minute. His body was sore all over, his shoulders protesting every swing of the pick. The others, he saw, fared little better even though they were accustomed to enduring the daily ordeal.

At long last Rufus said the words they were all waiting for. "That's enough for today. Toss your tools in the cart and let's go."

Fargo, on the verge of total exhaustion, plodded wearily to the surface. Holding the ball close to his chest with his forearms, he examined the many blisters scarring his palms. This time when the cool air struck him, he hardly noticed. Mechanically he plodded to the cabin on the heels of the rest, went inside, and sprawled on the bed.

"Don't doze off this soon," Haggerty advised him. "If you're asleep when they bring our grub, you won't get any supper."

Grunting, Fargo sat up, fighting off a wave of fatigue that promised to swamp him if he lapsed for a moment. His palms, he now saw, were even worse than he had believed. Both were bloody, the skin cracked in five or six spots where blisters had risen and been torn open by the motion of swinging the pick.

"Damn, those are bad," Haggerty said, coming over. "I wish I had something to give you, but they don't give us any medicine unless we're sick as dogs."

"Figures," Fargo mumbled.

Supper consisted of a bowl of tepid stew, almost-stale bread with butter, and weak coffee. Fargo ate greedily, polishing off his meal first. He was still famished when he was done, and his look of dissatisfaction drew a bitter laugh from Carson.

"Don't tell us you didn't get enough? This is a feast fit for a king." He swirled the broth with his spoon and added in disgust, "A dead king. Or a hog, because that's the only animal fit to eat this swill."

Rice nodded. "I'm so sick of this slop I can't stand it, but we either eat or we starve. They don't care. They can always find another poor soul to take the place of any one of us."

"They have to be stopped," Fargo said.

"Tell us something we don't know," Carson said. "We all want to shove a piece of ore down Traute's throat, but it's easier to talk about than to do."

Haggerty took a sip of coffee, a haunted look in his eyes. "When they first brought me here, I tried time and time again to get away. Tried everything I could think of. But they were too sharp for me, and they beat me bad after each attempt. Once Creel took a whip to my back and shredded the skin to where I couldn't lie on my back for two months. After a while I learned not to make them mad if I wanted to stay alive."

"So you gave up?" Fargo asked.

"No, I—" Haggerty replied, then caught himself and said, "Yes. I've got to be honest. They broke me. I gave up and haven't bothered to try in two years."

"We can't *let* them break us," Fargo said, gazing at

69

each of them in turn. "We're not animals to be kept caged the rest of our lives. If we work together, we can bust loose and make Traute pay for what he's done to us."

Carson shook his head. "You don't know what you're asking. You're new to this nightmare. You haven't given up hope like the rest of us."

"Does that mean you won't lend a hand when I make my play?"

"I can't speak for the others," Haggerty said, "only for myself. And I don't rightly know. I honestly don't know."

An uncomfortable silence fell on the room. None of the men met Fargo's gaze. Rising, he picked up the iron ball and rattled over to his bunk. He stared at the ball before putting it down, troubled that he had completely forgotten about it during the latter half of the day. In that short time he had become accustomed to having it attached to his leg, as if it was becoming part of him. How could he let that happen?

He let the ball fall with a thud, then sank onto his side and closed his eyes. Someone at the table was whispering, but he paid no heed. He began to review the events of the day, to go over the routine to see if there was any one time when the guards might be jumped. Fatigue flooded through him again, and try as he might he could not fend it off. Against his will he drifted to sleep.

The next morning the routine was repeated. Creel and Rufus rousted the prisoners out of bed, fed them hardtack and water, and took them to the mine entrance. Rufus stayed on top while Creel led them below. Unlike Rufus, who had kept his distance and rarely spoken, Creel hovered over them like a bird of prey, pouncing on any man who failed to do as good a job as he demanded. He cursed them, slapped them, treated them like scum. And they took it all in stride.

Except for Fargo. Inwardly he burned with an intense desire to smash Creel senseless. He bided his time, suffering abominably due to the constant agony in his hands. Then it happened. He swung the pick, and the handle slipped from his grasp and hit the wall.

"What the hell is the matter with you, saddle tramp?" Creel said, quickly coming over. "I didn't say you could put that tool down." Smirking, he jabbed the Trailsman in the side with the club.

Fargo snapped. All the anger he had pent up since being railroaded burst out of him. He felt the club strike his rib, felt the pain flare through his chest, and he sprang, his hands outstretched to fasten on the guard's thick neck.

7

The attack caught Creel flat-footed.

Fargo was on Creel before the bigger man could react, his fingers gouging deep into Creel's throat while his free leg swept up and in, smashing the guard in the stomach. Roaring in rage, Creel backpedaled and batted at Fargo's wrists with the club. Fargo clung fast, or tried to when suddenly he was pulled to the limit of the chain and jerked to a stop, weighted down by the heavy ball.

Creel raised the club on high for a blow at Fargo's head so Fargo let go and dropped flat, rolling to the right. He heard a loud thud as the club struck dirt. Glancing up at the irate giant, he swung his right leg in an arc, catching Creel on the knee. There was a distinct snap and the guard cried out, then flung the club aside and made a grab for his revolver.

Fargo kicked again, viciously driving his heel into the guard's other knee. Creel bellowed and fell forward, forcing Fargo to roll aside or be pinned. Surging to his knees, Fargo punched Creel on the jaw as the man cleared leather. Creel was dazed but not out; twisting, he tried to bring the gun to bear.

Fargo deflected the barrel with his left hand while lashing out with his right, his knuckles splitting Creel's lips open. The guard, even madder now, backhanded Fargo across the face and Fargo fell. He went to push up but he was too slow.

A wicked grin creased Creel's bloody mouth as the giant leveled the gun at Fargo's midsection. "Any last words, bastard?" he asked thickly, his eyes agleam with anticipation.

Fargo saw Creel's thumb tighten on the hammer. In a second a slug would rip through him like a hot knife. He tensed his right leg to kick when assistance came from an unexpected quarter.

Haggerty, tugging mightily on his ball and chain, hurled his frail frame at the giant, colliding with Creel's gun arm and knocking it against Creel's barrel chest. Haggerty desperately clung to the arm, thereby preventing the guard from firing.

"Get off, damn you!" Creel thundered. He shook his arm, failed to dislodge the old-timer, then rammed his other hand, balled into a massive fist, into Haggerty's gut. Gasping in torment, Haggerty toppled. Now free to do as he pleased, Creel swung toward Fargo, blood lust animating his features until he saw what was in Fargo's poised hands.

During those moments when the guard was distracted, Fargo had pushed to his knees, taken hold of his iron ball, and lifted it as high as he could. The instant that Creel turned, he bashed the ball into Creel's face with all the power in his muscular body.

The sound of the blow landing resembled that of a large rock crushing an overripe melon. Creel sagged, his arms going limp, his eyelids fluttering, a crimson geyser spraying from a crack in his forehead.

Fargo rose, raised the ball—at the very extent of its chain—and brought it sweeping down onto the top of the guard's head. There was a sickening crunch, then Creel fell on his face, his arms outflung. Fargo released the gore-spattered ball and wiped the back of his hand across his perspiring face. He suddenly realized he was breathing heavily. His limbs became strangely weak. Sinking into a crouch, he picked up Creel's gun and checked the cylinder. Five of the chambers contained cartridges.

"Sweet Jesus!" Haggerty exclaimed. "I never thought you could do it!"

Carson stepped forward, and before anyone could guess what he had in mind, he buried a pick in the giant's broad back. "That's for all the times you turned me black and blue, you son of a bitch!" he said, letting go of the handle. The pick jutted obscenely upward, its tapered point buried deep.

"What do we do now?" Rice asked.

"We take care of Rufus," Fargo replied. He glanced

at Haggerty. "Which one of them carries the key to our shackles?"

"I don't think either of them do. Used to be the key was always kept on a hook in their shack."

Fargo decided to be certain anyway. He searched Creel's pockets but found only a few coins, a few bills, and the makings for cigarettes. Removing Creel's gunbelt, he strapped it around his own waist.

"Why do you get the gun?" Carson asked. "Maybe one of us should have it."

"The Trailsman did the killin' so it's his," Haggerty said in Fargo's defense.

Rice had moved a few yards up the tunnel. "Do you think Rufus heard the ruckus? He might be waiting up there to pick us off as we come out."

"I doubt it," Fargo said. "We're too far down for him to have heard." He wedged the revolver under the gunbelt to the right of the buckle, then leaned over and picked up the iron ball once more. Assuming the lead, he hiked upward.

The others nervously followed, Haggerty and Yost carrying lanterns. All of their faces were pale in the yellow glow. No one spoke.

Fargo climbed steadily, warily. He could think of nothing else except getting his hands on the key. Freedom was what he craved more than anything, and once he was free he was going after Vincent Traute and the rest of the gang. They would never enslave anyone again, never put another man through the same torment he had experienced.

When at length he spied a glimmer of light far ahead, Fargo halted, then raised his right arm for the others to do likewise. "Blow out those lanterns," he directed and waited until they obeyed before advancing. He drew the pistol and cocked the hammer. The glimmer of light became a vertical patch of sunshine. Soon he could distinguish the timbers framing the entrance, and he slowed, hugging the left-hand wall.

Faintly he heard whistling. His left arm ached under the burden of the ball, but he dared not let it fall. The noise might be overheard. Keeping his back to the wall, he edged to within a foot of the opening and paused.

Radiant sunshine bathed the mountain, the cabin, and

the shack. Standing with his back to the mine, apparently enjoying the splendid view of the valley from his lofty perch, Rufus stood twenty feet away, his arms folded, tapping his right foot as he whistled a popular saloon tune.

Fargo took a step and paused again. He must give his eyes time to adjust to the light before revealing his presence. Rufus coughed and stared skyward but did not turn around. Just a few more seconds, Fargo reflected, and he would give the guard the surprise of his life. He inched outward, squinting in order to see.

At that instant Rufus casually swung toward the entrance. His eyes became the size of walnuts, his mouth slackened in astonishment. "What the hell!" he declared and went for his six-shooter.

A single shot was all it took, a bullet to the brain that spun Rufus around and dropped him before he could draw.

Fargo didn't bother to verify the guard was dead. He made straight for the shack, hurrying as best he was able, aware the sound of the gunshot would carry to the base of the mountain and beyond if the wind was right. Perhaps they would hear it in Serenity. Someone might come to investigate.

The door was unlocked. He threw it open to find a pigsty, with trash and partially eaten food littering the floor. Neither of the bunks were made. Dirty pans and tin cups formed a heaping pile on a table against a wall. He scanned the other walls and spotted a small metal hook from which hung an equally small key. Jamming the revolver under his belt again, he snatched the key loose and stepped outside.

"Did you find it?" Haggerty eagerly asked.

Placing the iron ball on the grass, Fargo swiftly inserted the slender key into the narrow hole on the shackle, gave a quick twist, and wanted to shout for joy when the shackle fell at his feet. He slowly straightened, feeling a tingle course down his spine, thrilled to be free at last.

"Me next," Carson said, joining them and grabbing for the key.

With a deft motion Fargo drew his hand back out of

reach. "Haggerty is next," he said, and gave their salvation to the old-timer.

Fargo smiled at the tears that formed in the old man's eyes. Haggerty's fingers trembled as he knelt and applied the key to the lock. Tears trickled over his grizzled cheeks when the shackle smacked to the earth. Laughing in delight, he stood and bestowed a look of supreme gratitude on Fargo. "I can never thank you enough, Trailsman," he said. "This is the happiest moment of my life."

In the forest below the shack a rifle cracked. A neat red hole blossomed in the center of the old man's chest, and Haggerty tottered backward in stupefied horror. He looked at Fargo, tried to form words, and pitched over.

"*No!*" Carson screamed. "Not now!"

From out of the pines poured horsemen, some with rifles, some with pistols, Traute and Ringald among them. A few snapped off shots, the bullets kicking up dirt near the prisoners.

One slug buzzed past Fargo, and in the blink of an eye he whirled and raced between the shack and the cabin, drawing his six-gun on the fly. He was in full stride once he broke into the open. Glancing back on hearing the pounding of onrushing hoofs, he saw Burke come around the corner of the shack and press a rifle to his shoulder. Fargo cut to the left and squeezed off two rapid shots.

Both rounds hit home. Uttering a strangled shriek, Burke threw his arms aloft, then tumbled.

The sight of Burke's horse thundering in his general direction gave Fargo the answer. He slid the pistol into its holster to free his hands and moved to intercept the animal. In a second it was right beside him and going past. He leaped, catching hold of the saddle horn, and threw his right leg onto the saddle. His blistered hands slipped though, before he could swing upright, and the next thing he knew the horse plunged into the forest and the limb of a pine tree slammed into his side.

He felt himself falling, hit his shoulder on a cushion of pine needles, and rolled to his feet. Already the fleeing horse was beyond his reach. He began to chase it anyway, then looked back on hearing more shots arise on the opposite side of the cabin.

Two riders materialized, neither of whom he knew.

Whirling, Fargo headed for deep cover, ducking down into a thicket as the horsemen attained the trees.

"Are you sure he went this way?" one of them said.

"You saw Burke lying there, didn't you?" countered his companion.

"He can't have gotten far then," said the first man.

"Doesn't matter how far he gets," said the other. "Once the boss sends for Cutler, the Trailsman is as good as dead."

They spread out, both alert, their weapons cocked, and passed the thicket, the closest rider not ten feet off.

Fargo was lying flat, concealed by branches and leaves, his eyes glued to the hoofs of the nearest horse as it went by. Waiting until the men had gone a dozen yards, he shoved into a crouch and studied the situation. There were angry yells back at the mine, but the shooting had stopped. With the rugged heights of the mountain to the west, the riders to the south, and more gunmen to the north, the sole avenue of escape left open to him was to the east, down the slope toward Serenity.

Turning on his heels, Fargo glided among the trunks of the firs and spruce until he had put a safe distance behind him. Then he rose and ran. He became winded much sooner than he ordinarily would have, yet pressed on. Twice he stumbled and almost fell. His battered body was aching all over when he came to a clearing hundreds of yards below the mine and halted.

He thought about Haggerty and scowled. The old man had never harmed a living soul, had never deserved the fate that befell him. Traute had more to pay for than ever before, and he resolved right then and there he wasn't leaving this valley until he put an end to the outlaw's reign of terror.

But that was putting the cart before the horse, Fargo realized. First he must save his own hide.

He ran on, skirting the clearing, and was close to the forest when he glanced down at the town and spied several riders galloping toward the base of the mountain. Even at that distance he was sure one of the riders wore buckskins and a dark hat.

It must be Jeff Cutler.

How long would it take Cutler to reach the mine, be filled in on what had happened, and begin tracking him?

Half an hour? Less? Somehow he must throw Cutler off the trail. But *how,* when Cutler was every bit as skilled as he was and knew every trick ever thought up?

Fargo covered another hundred yards while angling to the right. Swinging to the southeast would enable him to eventually circle around and approach the town from the south. Serenity was his first destination because there he would find the Ovaro and maybe his own guns. Then it was on to Traute's so-called ranch.

Behind him on the slope, from the vicinity of the mine, a single shot broke the stillness, and seconds later another single shot, to the south of the mine.

Signals? Fargo wondered. Had they begun their hunt for him without Cutler? He tried to put himself in Traute's place, to imagine what the man would do. He figured that by now all the prisoners had been rounded up and were probably back in the cabin. Those still alive, that was. Fargo guessed Traute had become impatient and ordered his men to fan out in all directions. Fargo hoped they would concentrate their search to the south of the mine, not to the east. Until Cutler arrived, they were little threat.

He unexpectedly burst from the pines and saw a chasm directly in front of him. He halted, sliding to a stop on the rim of the ravine too wide to leap across and too steep to descend. Cursing under his breath, he turned to the left, following the rim, hoping the ravine would end or he would find somewhere to safely cross. Meanwhile the slope slanted ever lower, and the trees became fewer and more spread out. He was losing his cover.

Then he spied the downed tree. A giant of the forest, struck by lightning as evidenced by the split down its middle and its many charred limbs, had been uprooted on his side of the ravine and toppled, the upper third coming to rest on the far rim.

Fargo reached the uprooted trunk and halted. This, he knew, was just what he had been looking for. Horses couldn't cross the makeshift bridge. Those after him would have to go all the way around the ravine, delaying them greatly. With a lot of luck and perseverance he could reach the other side and gain valuable time. It was too bad he wouldn't be there to see Cutler's face when the man arrived.

Grinning, Fargo gripped the stubby end of a broken root and carefully climbed up onto the top of the trunk. It was a yard wide, providing enough room to walk easily without fear of losing his balance, and there were ample handholds thanks to the many limbs although some of them were so brittle they broke at the slightest touch. He was compelled to go slowly, to test each limb before taking a step.

Halfway across he nearly lost his life.

Fargo had taken hold of a thick vertical limb and given it a shake to see how sturdy it was. Satisfied it was stout enough, he started to ease around it, turning his back to the yawning chasm below so as not to have to look down. Heights never bothered him, but he knew well that anyone might succumb to a brief dizzy sensation when gazing straight down from hundreds of feet up.

He got his left foot past the limb and was lifting his right leg to go all the way around when, taking him completely unaware, the limb broke off in his hand. The motion of the limb as it snapped off was slight, but more than enough to throw him off balance. His left foot suddenly slipped, and in an instant he was falling backward, his right arm outflung, his right foot having no purchase whatsoever.

Fargo did the only thing he could; he dived at the bottom of the limb where it was the thickest and seized hold with his left hand just as his left foot went out from under him. Both legs fell over the side. For harrowing seconds he hung there by one arm, his own weight and the force of gravity conspiring to send him to his death, until—with a tremendous heave—he grabbed another limb with his right hand.

A quick glance showed jagged boulders and rocks below. Steeling his muscles, he slowly pulled himself high enough to get his knees onto the trunk. Then, exercising infinite care, he stood, checked to make sure the pistol hadn't slipped loose, and continued crossing.

He breathed a sigh of grateful relief when he finally stepped off the downed tree onto firm soil. Looking back, he scanned the forest and the slope leading to the mine but saw no indication yet of pursuit. It wouldn't be long, though, before they showed up.

Below the ravine lay scattered trees amidst heavy

brush. He paced himself, not wanting to overexert his worn and weary body any more than he had to. Soon he came to a game trail, and rather than waste energy forcing his way through the brush, he stuck to the winding path until he was within fifty yards of the bottom of the mountain.

There he stopped to catch his breath. Severe pangs shot up and down his legs, and his lungs felt terribly sore. He sat on a flat rock, waiting until he felt fit enough to go on, and mulled over the best course of action to take once he reached Serenity.

The direct approach seemed the best. He was outnumbered, but most of the men working for Traute weren't lightning fast gunmen like Ringald or seasoned mountain men like Cutler. They were run-of-the-mill hardcases, neither too bright nor too deadly in their own right although collectively they were dangerous. The way he saw it, Traute, Ringald, and Cutler were the ones to worry about, the ones he must take care of first. For good measure he would also like to run into the phony marshal, Ward.

Five minutes of rest revitalized him enough to go on, and he now angled to the northeast so he could come up on the town from the south as he had planned. The trees and undergrowth thinned even more, and at times he had no choice but to cross open tracts where he was exposed to the clear view of anyone who might be seeking him from above.

The high grass covering the valley floor offered scant concealment. There were a few trees between the mountain and Serenity, but not enough to screen his approach. He had to move in a crouch, plowing through the grass from tree to tree until he drew within earshot of the town. He studied the fronts of the various buildings but detected no movement. For once there were no horses at the hitching posts, nor was the mongrel dog anywhere in sight.

From where he crouched Fargo couldn't see back to the ravine, but he did spot riders near where he believed he had crossed. Allowing for the time it would take them to go around the chasm, he had twenty minutes before they reached Serenity.

In a crouch he hastened to the last building at the

south end of the dusty street, the barn that served as a livery. Going to the back door, he opened it a crack and peered inside. Right away he saw the Ovaro in a stall. Evidently Traute had not gotten around to taking the pinto out to the ranch. He began to slip inside, then froze on hearing a strange sound, a low series of snorts such as grazing buffalo might make. Puzzled, he surveyed the interior and saw a pair of legs jutting out from an empty stall.

He pulled the revolver and moved forward on the balls of his feet. The legs turned out to belong to the piano player, Jeeter, who was passed out and snoring loudly, an empty bottle of whiskey clasped tightly in one arm, the bowler hat lying on straw beside him. The man was no threat and would likely be out for hours.

Fargo went to the large front doors and looked out. Still there was no one in evidence. He guessed that most of the men, including Marshal Ward, were up on the mountain. Jeeter, the two women, and possibly Griswald might be the only ones left in town. Thinking of the bartender caused his features to harden.

He hurried back to the Ovaro, gave it a pat, and quickly threw on his saddle blanket, saddle, and bridle. Taking the reins in his left hand, he boldly walked outside and made for the saloon. A puff of wind stirred the dust at his feet. Otherwise Serenity qualified as a ghost town, but appearances could be deceiving so he held his pistol cocked, his finger touching the trigger.

No one appeared, no one challenged him, and he halted in front of the saloon to tie the Ovaro to the post. Treading softly and staying to one side, he moved to the bat-wing doors. Three people were inside. Shirley and the other woman, a brunette, were seated at the long table eating a late breakfast. Near them, his body turned away from the entrance, stood Griswald.

Fargo smiled and let down the hammer on the gun. Wedging the barrel under his belt, he inched one of the doors open and slipped noiselessly inside. Neither of the women, engrossed in a conversation with Griswald, saw him. Clenching his fists, he tiptoed toward the barkeep.

"—knew that man was trouble from the minute I laid eyes on him," Griswald was saying. "Ten dollars says he's the reason there was all that shooting."

81

"I hope he gets away," Shirley declared.

"You would," Gloria said, sticking a forkful of scrambled eggs into her dainty mouth. Her eyes strayed past the bartender, and she abruptly stiffened.

Fargo knew what she was going to do before she did, and he took two long strides to reach Griswald before she did. He was still a yard away when her scream rent the air.

"Look out behind you!"

8

For a heavyset man who spent all his time indoors and seldom worked at anything harder than rearranging the tables and chairs, Griswald's reflexes were remarkable. He spun at the warning shout and brought his arms up protectively to shield his face and midsection.

Fargo's first punch failed to connect on the bartender's fleshy chin. Instead the blow was blocked, and immediately Griswald retaliated with a right cross that Fargo barely countered. He tried a left jab, missed, and received a fist in the ribs that sent pain shooting through his chest. Pivoting, he feinted. Griswald took the bait, and Fargo slammed home a punch to the jaw that lifted Griswald off his heels and sent the bartender crashing onto the long table.

"Get him!" Gloria shrieked.

Fargo could ill afford a prolonged fight. Every second was vital, what with Traute's men closing in on him. He leaped at Griswald but was knocked back by a foot on his torso. Then the bartender jumped up, fists held defensively, and fixed a baleful stare at him.

"You made a mistake coming back here, mister. But your mistake is my gain. Mr. Traute will pay me a considerable bonus for turning you over to him."

"You'll never collect."

Griswald waded in, swinging furiously, as Fargo backpedaled, ducking and dodging, trying not to dwell on the seconds ticking by. He could easily have drawn the revolver and shot the bartender dead, but Griswald was unarmed. And the shot just might be heard by the men near the bottom of the mountain and spur them to reach Serenity sooner.

Fargo dropped under a straight right to the head and scored with a right to Griswald's stomach, which was more muscular than he had supposed. The barkeep barely slowed. Fargo slipped outside a powerful left, then resorted to a trick he had learned the hard way years ago in a violent tavern brawl. He flicked a left jab at Griswald's moon of a face, and naturally Griswald raised his left fist to counter it. At the very last instant Fargo whipped the jab over Griswald's fist and speared his left thumb into Griswald's eye.

The bartender winced and backed up, instinctively pressing a hand to the injured eye, concerned for his sight at the expense of his safety.

Fargo had no compunctions about raining a right-left combination on Griswald's jaw. The portly man buckled as if his legs were made of wax, and he lay wheezing on the floor.

"Damn you!" Gloria said, her brown eyes flashing. "You hurt him!"

Ignoring her, Fargo stepped up to the table and addressed Shirley. "This is the chance you've been waiting for. Come with me, now, and I'll get you safely out of the valley."

"Now?" Shirley said.

"Right this minute. We have to hurry. I can have a horse saddled in no time."

"But all my things, all my clothes—"

"What about St. Louis? Or was that just talk?"

Shirley was in turmoil. She bit her lower lip, glanced at her friend, then at Fargo.

He tried one final time, saying, "I've got to get you away before the gunplay starts. I don't want you caught in the cross fire." He paused. "If you want, we'll take Gloria along."

The older woman vigorously shook her head. "You're not taking me anywhere. I'm no fool. Traute will track you down and kill you." She looked meaningfully at Shirley. "And anyone who is with you. He's not the forgiving sort."

"But you've told me time and time again you want to leave," Shirley said.

"Sure I do. But not until I can be certain of living long enough to reach the settlements."

"Please—" Shirley began.

Fargo interrupted brusquely. "There's no time for this.

Make up your mind. I'm leaving." He headed for the doorway, then paused, watching Shirley wrestle with her indecision. After a bit she nodded and stood.

"Maybe I'm the fool," she said to Gloria, "but I may never have a chance like this again. I truly don't much care what Traute will do to us if he catches us. I can't go on living as his slave. I'd rather die."

"You just might."

Fargo motioned for Shirley to join him, and together they hastened out to the hitching post. He mounted the pinto, then leaned down and gave her a hand in climbing up behind him. Her breasts rubbed against his back, her thighs against his legs as he turned the Ovaro and rode toward the livery. They were passing the marshal's office when he realized he was overlooking something and drew rein sharply.

"What's wrong?" Shirley asked.

"We need guns," Fargo said, twisting so he could lift his left leg clear over the Ovaro's neck and slide to the ground. "Stay there. I'll be right back."

The door was unlocked, the office tidy but heavy with dust except on the desktop and the chair. Fargo walked to a cabinet on the wall and grinned happily on finding the Sharps and the shotgun Ward had used in the saloon. Taking both, he stepped to the desk and opened all the drawers. His gunbelt and Colt were in one. Lying beside them was the toothpick.

When he exited the marshal's office he felt like a new man. His own pistol hung on his hip, his own rifle in his left hand, and his boot hid his throwing knife. He gave the shotgun and a box of shells to Shirley and climbed up.

A short trot brought them to the barn, where Shirley stood watch while Fargo attended to saddling a mare. Jeeter snoozed the whole time. Once she was up, Fargo forked leather and galloped eastward. As yet there was no sign of Traute's gang, leading him to conclude it had taken the outlaws longer than he figured to skirt the ravine. A stroke of luck for him.

They pushed their mounts, riding side by side, Shirley's long tresses blowing in the wind, her dress swirling up over her thighs. She rode extremely well, and Fargo made a comment to that effect.

"I did a lot of riding when I was a girl," she responded, and grinned wryly. "Since then I've been keeping my legs in practice."

"And doing a right fine job, if you don't mind me saying so."

Shirley laughed, her face aglow with the joy of being on the verge of gaining her freedom. She turned hooded eyes on him and said throatily, "If you pull this miracle off, I'll never be able to thank you properly."

"I'm sure you'll think of something."

No one else appeared on the trail to the gorge. They saw a few head of cattle, a few head of horses, and once a few black-tailed deer that bounded off into dense cover. Overhead puffy white clouds sailed through the blue sky at a leisurely pace.

"It's all so peaceful out here," Shirley remarked. "I'd almost forgotten what it can be like."

Repeatedly Fargo gazed back at Serenity, expecting to see a pack of riders materialize sooner or later. Inexplicably none did. He didn't know quite what to make of their absence. Was there, he wondered, another way out of the valley, a shortcut he didn't know about? He asked Shirley.

"Not that I've ever heard of, lover. And I would know after all this time."

Fargo could only pray she was right and that they wouldn't ride into an ambush. The gorge was his main worry. If Traute's band should know how to reach the top, the two of them would be blasted to shreds.

All appeared as it should when they got there. A chipmunk darted from one boulder to another, sparrows flitted playfully on the left side, and a rabbit bounded away as they drew close. The wildlife reassured Fargo that no one else was nearby, but he still held the Sharps in front of him with his thumb on the hammer as he entered the defile.

The air became warmer thanks to the reflection of sunlight off the sheer rock walls. A profound silence enveloped them, and in that silence the clumping of their animals seemed unnaturally loud.

Fargo constantly scanned both rims, his body tensed like a coiled spring. When, none too soon to suit him, they emerged into the open, he felt the tension drain from him. He reined up, debating their next move.

If they stuck to the trail, the outlaws might overtake them. His stallion was capable of outrunning practically any horse that lived, but Shirley's mare didn't possess the same speed and stamina. It would be better to find somewhere to hide out so they could lay low for a day or two. Then would come the final reckoning with Vincent Traute.

Accordingly he turned to the north, into the forest, and led Shirley mile after mile through an unending sea of evergreens broken intermittently by stands of regal aspens. He avoided valleys and meadows where the softer soil would more readily bear hoof prints, and he avoided high ground until they had gone over ten miles and found themselves at the base of a mountain. The slope offered a convenient spot to check their back trail, so up he went to a clearing where there was an unobstructed view of the surrounding countryside.

He intently scanned the forest of green stretching to the south and spotted a pair of elks in a grassy area a quarter of a mile off. But he saw no riders anywhere. Mystified, he waited a full five minutes, positive that Traute's gang couldn't be all that far behind. Yet they failed to appear.

Clucking the pinto into motion, he changed direction, now bearing to the northeast into a more rugged and remote region. He desired to put as much distance behind them as he could before night descended. Twilight had blanketed the land when they stopped for the day in a picturesque glade flanked by a bubbling creek.

Fargo let Shirley rest while he unsaddled both horses, rubbed them down with handfuls of grass, and ground-hitched them where they had easy access to the water. Next he gathered enough broken pine boughs to make a crude but serviceable lean-to. Last of all he collected enough dry wood for a very small fire. By then darkness had claimed the Rockies.

"I'm sorry I didn't have time to rustle up a rabbit or something for supper," Fargo said as they both sat next to the crackling flames. "There is some jerked venison in my saddlebags, if that will do."

Shirley had rarely spoken since leaving the gorge. All

day her expression had alternated between dreamy contentment and thoughtful deliberation. What she had been thinking about, Fargo had no idea. Now she looked at him and gave a warm smile. "I'm really not hungry."

"Care for some coffee?"

"Not at the moment." She sidled next to him and their shoulders touched. "I'm too excited as it is. I'm finally free! Do you have any idea what that means?"

Fargo thought of his excruciating ordeal in the mine and nodded. "Yes, I reckon I do."

"Then you should be able to figure out how much what you have done means to me," Shirley said, resting a gentle hand on his forearm. "I'd like to show my appreciation the only way I know how."

"You don't have to. I did it because it needed doing."

"I want to," she insisted.

Fargo sat still as her warm lips touched his and her silken tongue slid into his mouth. Making love had been the last thing on his mind, and it took a moment for him to realize that was her intention. He mentally weighed whether doing so was safe and decided the outlaws must be miles away if they hadn't lost the trail entirely. Traute, he reasoned, had probably stopped for the night, too, since only a fool or a madman risked crippling his horse by riding in the dark over unfamiliar mountainous terrain.

He responded with ardor to her kiss, his tongue dancing with her as his hands came up to cup her breasts. Through the material he could feel her nipples harden. She uttered a low moan and worked her mouth as if trying to suck him into her throat. Leaving one hand to massage her globes, he lowered his other hand to her thighs and slowly stroked them.

Somewhere to the west a wolf howled.

Fargo could feel the warmth of the fire on his face and the heat from her womanhood on his hand. He eased her down onto her back, then reclined on his side and applied his mouth to hers. She put both arms on his shoulders, her eyes mere slits, her sensuous form pressing against his as they fully embraced.

Their last lovemaking had been intensely passionate, conducted in the heat of carnal desire. This time it was different. Both of them took their time, savoring each moment, delighting in the pleasurable sensations the other aroused. Their kisses lingered on/and on. They dallied at foreplay, she using her expert fingers to excite his manhood, he using his lips and hands to mold her yielding flesh as he saw fit.

Her breasts were heaving, her legs opening and closing in silent invitation, when Fargo commenced removing her clothes, taking his sweet time about it, pausing often to nibble and lick her exposed skin. When he had her completely naked, he drew back on one elbow and regarded her exquisitely beautiful form as if it was a priceless work of art.

The firelight played over her smooth complexion, her cherry red nipples, her flat tummy, her willowy legs. The dark triangle at the junction of her legs was a sharp contrast. When she moved, her breasts swayed slightly but lost none of their uplifted contours. She was delectable, a feast for the eyes, and Fargo drank in the sight of her as would a man dying of thirst in the desert drink in the sight of an oasis.

He swooped his mouth to a nipple and tweaked it with his eager tongue, then gave the other nipple the same treatment. Slowly he eased downward, licking and nibbling a path across her stomach then around it until he inhaled her sweet scent. She lifted her head to gaze wonderingly at him, her eyes widening in rapturous surprise when his mouth descended and he sought the core of her sex.

Her hips bucked off the ground when his tongue probed deep. A groan burst from her throat. She thrashed her head from side to side and took hold of his hair, trying to push him in deeper, her thighs clamped to his head like a blacksmith's vise. She said something but the words were unintelligible.

Fargo licked her moist tunnel and flicked the tiny knob above it, sending tremors rippling through her entire body. She squirmed and ground herself into him so hard he could barely breathe. His left hand roamed over her soft buttocks while his right hand rubbed her stomach and back, his fingers crinkling the skin and leaving red marks in their wake.

Shirley's mouth shaped into a perfect oval. She cooed like a dove, her breasts like pale cantaloupes, her toes digging into the earth as she worked her legs back and forth. Lost in ecstasy, she spurted her inner juices again and again.

At length Fargo raised up to strip off his shirt, gunbelt, and pants. Spreading her legs wide, he knelt then slowly inched in until they were joined. She gasped, dug her nails into his arms, and trembled uncontrollably.

In the night an owl hooted.

Fargo placed his hands on her hips, held tight, and began pumping his hips. The friction heightened their lust. They both closed their eyes to better enjoy the feeling. He had no trouble controlling himself and pumped for minutes on end, all the while squeezing her breasts and kneading her tummy. For her part, she clawed at his back and occasionally gouged her nails into his buttocks.

They established a gentle rhythm and stuck to it. The cool breeze caressed them both. Around them the pines rustled. Nearby the horses grazed, the sounds of their munching mingling with the bubbling of the creek. Stars twinkled above.

Fargo got his fingers under Shirley's behind and lifted her a few inches off the ground for better leverage and penetration. Increasing his tempo, he also increased the force of his strokes, producing the desired effect almost immediately.

Shirley clung to him as would a drowning woman to a lifeboat, her hips glued to his, her legs wrapped securely around his waist, wrapped tighter than his belt would be. She met each thrust with a counterthrust of her own, responding to his ardor and doing her utmost to give him as much pleasure as she was getting from him.

The night blurred, the sounds diminished. All Fargo could see was her flushed face, and all he could hear was her panting breaths. A tingling at the base of his spine told him the explosion was building, and he moved even faster in anticipation. She knew. Together they attained the pinnacle of red-hot passion, and they both came simultaneously.

Fargo arched his back and gripped her hard when the eruption tore through him, his manhood plowing into the depths of her tunnel. Their stomachs smacked loudly together. The force of his coming lifted her bottom up off the grass, and she uttered a drawn-out whine, her eyelids quivering, her legs trying to squeeze the life out of him.

"Oh, yes! Oh! Ohhhhhh!"

Spent, they gradually coasted to a stop. He lay on top of her, her breasts mashing into his chest, her legs slack under his. He kissed her lightly, then smiled when she nuzzled under his chin and licked his neck. Her fingers played in his beard.

"You have a talent," she said.

"I do?"

"Don't play innocent with me. You're the best damned lover I've ever had."

"Care to put that on paper?"

Shirley giggled and gave him a hug. "You're different from most, Trailsman. You make a woman feel free to do what she wants with you, and for that I thank you." She paused. "I doubt a man like you will ever marry, not when you can have the pick of any filly you want. I'll bet you've had more than your fair share, too. As handsome as you are, they must line up and take turns. Am I right?"

"You talk too much."

"I like to talk after making love. Don't you?"

"I'd rather sleep."

"Typical. Most men get what they want, then they roll over and act as if the woman isn't there."

"I thought you just said I was different from most?" Fargo responded and winced when she impishly bit his shoulder.

For a while she said nothing, then: "What about tomorrow? Something tells me that you're not going to ride off and leave Traute to carry on as he had been doing. What are your fixing to do next?"

"We'll talk about it in the morning."

"I'm worried, is all. I don't want anything to happen to you."

"It won't."

"You can't be certain. And if it does, where does that leave me? I could never find my way to Denver or anywhere else all by myself. With my luck I'd run into a grizzly or a bunch of hostiles."

Sighing, Fargo rolled off her and propped his arm on the ground so they were eye-to-eye. "What will happen,

91

will happen, and all the fretting in the world won't change things. Yes, I'm going back. I have to. I owe it to Haggerty."

"Old Tom Haggerty? What's he mean to you?"

"They killed him."

"Oh."

She fell silent, allowing Fargo to lie by her side and close his eyes. He knew he should get dressed, but he liked the touch of her warm skin and the breeze on his body. Soon he was drowsy, and against his will he fell asleep.

It seemed like only a minute later, although he immediately sensed much more time had elapsed, that a gust of cold air woke him up. He realized the fire had gone out, and he could tell that Shirley had pulled on her dress and was lost in dreamland. Shivering, he sat up and gazed at the bulky outlines of the horses, ensuring both were there. Then he swiftly tugged into his buckskins, strapping on the Colt last.

The Trailsman retrieved his blanket so he could cover both of them. Lying on his back, he rested his head on his forearm and stared at the heavens. The questions Shirley had asked nagged at him, bothering him, and he reflected on what he should do. It would be best for her if he took her to Denver and then came back. But there was no telling what Traute would do to the men at the mine in the meantime. He wouldn't put it past the four-flusher to have all the prisoners killed so there wouldn't be anyone to speak against him should Fargo return with the army.

He gave careful attention to the problem until his thoughts strayed and his weary body drew him into a deep sleep. Vague dreams filtered through his mind, only snatches of which he recollected when bright sunlight on his face awakened him an hour after sunrise. He lay still, aware of Shirley at his side, and chided himself for oversleeping. They should have been up and in the saddle at first light. And he wasn't the only one who thought so, because a second later a cold, mocking voice caused his stomach muscles to involuntary constrict.

"About time you woke up, Trailsman. I can't see how a lazy varmint like you got such a fierce reputation

92

when you sleep half the day through. When do you find time for killing all the polecats and such that cross your path?"

Fargo turned and stared into the menacing barrel of a rifle held in the hands of the renegade mountain man named Jeff Cutler.

9

Any man who wanted to survive for long on the raw frontier quickly learned certain essential lessons: never ride in the open during a lightning storm; never make a big campfire in hostile territory; never argue with a long-haired, whiskey-drinking liar; and never make any sudden moves when looking down the barrel of an enemy's gun.

So Fargo held himself perfectly still, his hands folded on his chest, waiting for Cutler to make the next move. He knew the mountain man could easily have shot him from concealment, which led him to believe that Cutler must have a reason for taking him alive, a reason which wasn't hard to guess.

"At least I didn't catch you with your britches down," Cutler said, chuckling. He glanced at Shirley, who was still sleeping, and the corners of his mouth turned down. "Too bad about her. She's always treated me decent."

"What do you mean?" Fargo asked.

"You know damn well what I mean," Cutler said. "Traute is almost as mad at her as he is at you." He brightened again. "Almost, but not quite. Ain't never seen anyone as riled as that man. He'll likely peel your hide from you with a butcher knife, then feed you to the buzzards."

"How close is he?"

"Hell, he's back in Serenity, waiting for me to fetch you. Probably sitting in the saloon right this minute, drinking and planning on how he's going to rub you out." Cutler took a stride backward, the rifle held steady and true. "You should have seen him when we got to town and he found out you'd escaped with the girl. He ranted and raved and slapped Griswald around. Nothing calmed him down until he strung up Jeeter."

"He hanged the liveryman?"

Cutler nodded. "There was no call for it, far as I could see. Jeeter was so drunk he could hardly stand up. Ringald must have felt the same way because he objected to the notion. But Traute wouldn't listen to anyone. He had some of his men string Jeeter up from a beam in the barn. Said it would serve as a lesson to the others."

Shirley mumbled and shifted position.

"Traute made a mistake, if you ask me," Cutler went on amiably. "Now most of those men will skip out the first chance they get. No one in his right mind likes to work for a rabid wolf. You never know when the wolf will turn on you." He wagged the barrel. "Enough socializing. I want you to get to your knees, real slow like, and use your thumb and one finger to lift that hog-leg out of your holster. Set it down on the ground just as slow." He paused. "I reckon I don't need to tell you what will happen if you try anything fancy."

Fargo did as he was told, exaggerating each movement so Cutler could plainly see he wasn't anxious to commit suicide. Once the gun was deposited, Cutler made him stand and move to one side.

"It sort of surprised me when you didn't light out for Denver," Cutler commented as he stepped forward. Keeping the rifle trained on Fargo, he crouched and picked up the Colt. "I gather you were fixing to go pay Traute a visit once you had Shirley safe. Am I right?"

"It seemed like a good idea at the time."

"I would have done the same thing if I was in your boots," Cutler said, rising and moving around Shirley until he stood close to her head. He poked her shoulder with his rifle and said, "Rise and shine, beautiful. I'm afraid you're in for a bad day."

Smacking her lips as if she were eating sweets, Shirley touched a hand to the spot the barrel had pressed against but her eyes remained closed.

"Sleeps like a log," Cutler said, poking her again, only harder this time.

Slowly Shirley's eyes fluttered open. "What?" she said sleepily. "What's going on? Did you say something, Skye?"

"No, I did," Cutler informed her.

Suddenly Shirley saw him, and she came up off the

ground as if shot from a cannon. Then she saw Fargo, his arms held out from his sides, his fingers spread wide, and gasped. "Oh, no!"

"Sorry, darling," Cutler said. "But I have a job to do. I was told to track the two of you down and bring you back to Traute. Had to ride all night to get here, but it was worth it."

"You could let us go if you wanted," Fargo said, grasping at straws. "You're not like Traute and the rest of them. I can tell. Just go back and say you couldn't find us and let it go at that."

"I doubt very much Traute would believe me. He knows how good I am," Cutler said. "Besides, I couldn't do it even if I was of a mind to. I gave my word I'd fetch you, and fetch you I will." Tilting his head back, he pursed his lips and gave a loud whistle. There was a loud crackling in the underbrush to the north, and seconds later Cutler's dun appeared, trotting up to its master and nuzzling his back.

"Taught the critter myself," Cutler bragged with a grin. Moving to the side, he removed a rope from the saddle and tossed the rope at Shirley's feet. "Do me a favor, darling, and tie Fargo's hands behind his back nice and tight. We have a long ride ahead of us, and I don't want him getting any funny notions about jumping me when I'm not looking."

"I'll be damned if I will!" Shirley snapped.

"Oh, you'll do it, all right," Cutler said, "or I'll bash your teeth in. Traute wants you alive, but he didn't say you had to be delivered without a scratch."

Shirley hesitated only a moment before snatching up the rope and coming over to Fargo. "Forgive me," she said.

Resigned to the inevitable, Fargo swung his arms to the small of his back and let her do as Cutler wanted. She looped the rope about his wrists twice, leaving enough slack for him to work his hands loose, and was about to secure a knot when Cutler spoke harshly.

"Make damn sure it's tight, woman. I'm going to check, and if it ain't, you'll suffer."

Fargo heard her sigh, then felt the loops tighten, pinching his skin. She did a proper job this time, so much so that he would be unable to free himself without strenuous effort—or the aid of the Arkansas toothpick. He kept expecting Cutler to take the knife from his boot, but Cutler gave no indication he knew the throwing knife was there. Then Fargo remembered the mountain man hadn't been present when he was knocked out, captured, and searched. Unless Traute had thought to mention it specifically, Cutler was unaware Fargo carried the blade.

"Now both of you can sit down," Cutler directed when Shirley was done. Once they complied, he went to their horses, brought over both animals, and hastily saddled them. The Ovaro gave him problems by fidgeting and shying, upset at being handled by a stranger, but soon the mountain man had all three horses set to go.

"If you behave yourselves you'll reach Serenity without a scratch," Cutler said, walking up to them. "But if you give me so much as a lick of trouble, I won't hesitate to make you regret it." He prodded Shirley with his gun. "You fork leather first. Try running off and I'll shoot him."

"I never knew you could be so coldhearted," Shirley taunted as she climbed on her animal. "Fargo's wrong. You fit right in with Traute and his crowd. You're as ruthless as they are."

"No, the Trailsman is right. There was a time, back when my wife and younguns were alive, that I would have told Traute to go kiss a grizzly if he asked me to work for him. I was the most peaceable man on earth except when set upon." His features darkened. "Their dying twisted my innards so bad I could scarcely stand living. I'm a mite ashamed to admit I went downhill fast. Now I just don't give a damn about anything."

"You can't—" Shirley began.

"Enough jawing!" Cutler said bitterly. "All this jabbering is getting me mighty upset. I don't want another word out of either of you unless I say you can talk."

They all mounted and headed toward the valley, Shirley in front, Fargo in the middle, and Cutler in the rear so he could keep both of them covered.

Fargo had to guide the pinto using his legs alone, a simple enough task since he had ridden the stallion for so long it responded superbly to the least little pressure. With Cutler behind him he dared not work on the rope binding him; all he could do was ride and think. He wondered if the mountain man would push them on to Serenity without stopping, or whether they would be permitted to rest once or twice. Their lives depended on the latter.

They traversed the same terrain they had the day before. Several times Cutler had to tell Shirley she was straying to the east or the west and get her back on track. The day was a scorcher, the merciless sun beating down on them, the temperature climbing exceptionally high, well into the nineties.

About noon, as they entered a clearing, Shirley glanced over her shoulder and called out, "Can we take a breather? I'm bushed." Then she added, almost as an afterthought, "You never did let us eat any breakfast."

"I reckon we can," Cutler said. "I'm hungry myself. Haven't eaten a bite since I cut out after you."

Fargo managed to swing down without help and stepped to a log lying close to the encircling trees. Taking a seat, he stretched his legs and watched Cutler tether their horses. Shirley was fussing with her hair. He saw Cutler glance at him, then turn to the dun. For a few seconds he was preoccupied with opening his saddlebags, and it was all the distraction Fargo needed. He girded himself, about to rise and race into the pines, when Shirley ruined his plan addressing him loudly.

"I doubt Jeff is about to let me untie you, so I'll feed you if you have no objections."

Fargo had to answer. If he didn't, if he ran, Cutler would look around to see why he hadn't responded, and he'd lose the four or five seconds head start he needed to accomplish what he had in mind. "Fine," he said and saw the mountain man turn.

"I have six biscuits here. Made them myself, and they're not half bad. Care to have one?"

"Don't mind if I do," Shirley said. "I'm so starved I could eat your horse."

Cutler gave two of the biscuits to her, and she came over to sit beside Fargo. "Open wide," she said, holding a biscuit up to his lips. As he bit down, she lowered her voice and whispered, "I saw you tense up. What were you fixing to do? Run off and leave me?"

Chewing heartily, Fargo bobbed his chin once.

"Are you loco? Cutler will be right after you. And

there's no telling what he'll do to me to make sure I don't try to escape while he's chasing you."

"He won't hurt you," Fargo said softly, barely moving his lips.

"In the frame of mind he's in, I wouldn't put anything past him. He's liable to shoot my leg out from under me just so I'll stay put."

"He might tie you up. That's all."

"Do you have one of them crystal balls in your pocket? You don't know for certain what he'll do."

"I know he won't."

"Listen, Fargo. I don't aim to get myself shot if you're wrong. Please don't try anything."

"If I don't," Fargo said, "we're both dead once he gets us to Serenity. Is that what you want?"

She lifted the biscuit, anxiety etching her face, crow's-feet accenting her eyes. "Of course not."

"Then be ready at any time. I don't know when my next chance will come, so I won't have time to warn you. Just do whatever he says to do and you'll be fine," Fargo said, and saw her stiffen as they both heard footsteps.

Cutler was walking toward them. "What are the two of you whispering about? I don't take kindly to having this chatter going on behind my back."

"We're passing the time of day," Shirley said brazenly.

"Then why whisper?" Cutler demanded suspiciously.

"You said we couldn't talk, remember? We didn't want you bashing our brains out."

Fargo had to admire her courage. She didn't even flinch as Cutler loomed over her with close scrutiny as if he was trying to read the truth in the set of her features.

"I still might if I find you're lying to me, darling," Cutler told her. "But I reckon it's all right for the two of you to jaw a spell. At least that way I'll know what you're saying."

"Thank you," Shirley said.

Taking a step backward, Cutler sank to his knees and munched on a biscuit for a minute. Then, looking at Fargo, he commented, "For the life of me, I can't figure out how you let a tinhorn like Traute get his hooks into you. Didn't your nose tell you that something was wrong with that setup when you rode in?"

"I wanted to get the man who killed Charlie Pitman."

Cutler stopped chewing. "I didn't much like doing that. Charlie was all right in my book."

"Then why?"

"Why else? Money. I rode into Serenity about six months ago. They were aiming to railroad me until I happened to mention my name. I guess one or two of them had heard of me. The next thing I knew, Traute himself showed up and asked me to go to work for him. Promised me more money each week than I used to make in a year. And he's been as good as his word."

The information was a revelation, causing Fargo to wonder if he had made a mistake in not mentioning his full name when he first walked into the saloon. If he had, they might have left him alone. The only one he had told was Shirley, and the name had meant nothing to her until later, after Cutler recognized him and the word spread around town. He stared at the mountain man. "Is it worth it?" he asked. "Selling your soul for a few handfuls of silver?"

The backhanded blow was a streak, catching Fargo full on the right cheek and knocking him off the log. He fell onto his side, his cheek stinging but otherwise unhurt, and looked up to see Cutler drawing back a foot to kick him while he was down.

"Jeff, no!" Shirley cried.

Cutler froze, his leg half cocked, his skin as scarlet as a mountain sunset. "What do you know?" he bellowed at Fargo. "Who the hell are you to sit in judgment on me? If it happened to you, if you lost all I did, do you think you would act any different?"

"I can't say," Fargo admitted.

The anger slowly drained out of Cutler, and he sullenly lowered his leg. Hefting his rifle, he tramped in a small circle, letting off steam, then he abruptly confronted them. "Mount up. We're riding."

"So soon? I'm still hungry," Shirley protested.

"You'll be a lot hungrier before the day is done," Cutler snarled, grabbing her wrist and hauling her erect. "Now do as I say before I really lose my temper."

They resumed riding in a single file. Once again Cutler held the rear position, only now he was morose and surly, barking at them whenever he urged them to go faster or to issue directions. He had the air of a man who keenly wanted to kill someone and wasn't too particular about who it might be.

Fargo casually glanced back every so often, hoping Cutler would let down his guard, but he was disappointed. He could almost feel Cutler's eyes boring into his back every step of the way. The man watched him continually, perhaps hoping he would make a bid for freedom so he could be shot down on the spot, Traute or no Traute. His attempt to appeal to Cutler's conscience in the hope the man would release them had done the exact opposite; now Cutler was out for his blood.

Mile after mile fell behind them, the sun arcing steadily higher. The afternoon waned. It became clear they wouldn't reach Serenity before nightfall, but Cutler wasn't about to make camp. They'd keep going until they reached the town.

Fargo realized he would have to take a desperate gamble and try to strike back at Cutler even if they didn't stop, and he patiently waited for the sun to set, knowing the darkness would work in his favor.

Twilight blanketed the Rockies when Shirley shifted and yelled back to Cutler, "Please can we call a halt? I need a rest."

"No."

"What harm can it do to stop for fifteen minutes? That's all I ask."

"No."

"Damn you. Is this any way to treat a friend? We were drinking partners once."

"Not any more. And if you open your mouth again, I'll shut it so that you won't be able to talk for a month."

Muttering under her breath, Shirley faced forward and rode with her shoulders slumped in dejection.

Gradually the sun settled below the western horizon, disappearing behind a snow-crowned peak. Vivid hues of red, orange, and pink colored the sky.

Fargo marked the lengthening of the shadows to gauge when he should make his move while surreptitiously flexing his arm and legs muscles over and over so he would be ready. He was afraid the tight rope might cut off the circulation to his hands, but the repeated flexing prevented their becoming numb.

The majestic sunset faded and was replaced by the gathering night. A few stars gleamed like distant lanterns. To the east a half moon rose, casting a pale radiance over the murky forest.

They rode into a spacious valley and crossed a grass-covered meadow. To their right an elk snorted and bolted into the brush, its great bulk dimly visible for a fleeting moment before it vanished. At the far side the trees and undergrowth formed a tangle of gloomy vegetation. Shirley made for a gap between two forest giants, her horse plodding wearily.

There would never be a better time, Fargo decided, vigorously working his fingers back and forth. He pretended to relieve a cramp in his neck by stretching and turning his head from side to side, his real motive being to see how far back Cutler rode and to notice how he was holding the rifle. The mountain man held the gun loosely in the crook of his left elbow. To fire, Cutler must swing the barrel down and around while wedging the stock to his shoulder, which would take a second or two depending on how fast Cutler reacted. It wasn't much of an edge, but it was all Fargo knew he would get.

Shirley's ghostlike figure was ten feet ahead when the Ovaro reached the tree line. Fargo quickly slipped his boots from the stirrups, coiled his leg muscles, and, as he passed a tall pine bearing low limbs that nearly touched the ground, he vaulted from the saddle. His right shoulder hit hard, jarring his spine but doing no real damage, and he lithely rolled to his feet and bolted, hearing Cutler vent an oath as he darted around the pine.

Pounding hoofs warned him the mountain man had started to give chase, then the pounding stopped. Cutler must be in a quandary, trying to figure out what to do about Shirley. Fargo hunched low, weaving among the trees, counting on the darkness to shroud him from Cutler's view. The boom of a rifle split the night, and a slug ripped through a thicket on his left.

Suddenly he came to a drop-off and went over the edge running before he could stop. It was only eight feet to the bottom, the slope not all that steep, so he was able to stay upright the whole way down, dirt spraying from under his boots. Once on firm footing, he bore to the left.

He heard them coming then, heard horses being pushed recklessly through the woods, and figured Cutler had ordered Shirley to follow or else suffer the consequences. Was one of them leading the Ovaro or had they left the stallion behind? They were twenty yards to his rear, nearing the drop-off. Again he cut to the left, making a loop back to where he had jumped from the saddle, placing each foot down as quietly as possible and avoiding branches that might snag his buckskins.

The pinto was gone. Fargo figured they had taken it. He moved into the trees beyond, crouched at the base of a wide trunk, and stuck his finger under his boot to grab the toothpick. The knife slid out with ease. Grasping the hilt, he carefully reversed his hold until the razor edge of the blade rested against the rope binding his wrists. Applying pressure, he began a slow sawing motion.

West of him the undergrowth crackled as Cutler searched diligently. As near as Fargo could tell, there was just one horse moving about. What had happened to Shirley? And where was the Ovaro? Anxious for her safety, he sawed faster and faster. Once the hilt slipped, and he nearly lost his grip.

The rope was thick, the strands difficult to slice, but he persisted until he guessed he had cut a third of the way through. Relaxing his hands, he bunched his shoulders and exerted all of his strength in an attempt to snap the rope in two. The rope held. Frustrated, he resumed slicing.

Suddenly Fargo lifted his head and listened intently, surprised to discover the woodland cloaked in silence. The sounds of the moving horse had ceased. He turned on his knees and peered along his back trail but saw no movement. Where the hell was Cutler? he wondered, redoubling his efforts to cut free. Had the mountain man dismounted to try and track him? Tracking at night was extremely difficult, requiring skill few men possessed, but he wouldn't put it past Cutler to be one of the few.

Fargo's fingers ached, his wrists were sore, and several times the tip of the knife nicked his arms. He felt a trickle of blood but refused to stop. More strands parted.

Once more he tried to break his bonds and failed. Annoyed at the delay and heedless of the risk, he slashed furiously, wincing when the point nicked him again. Abruptly, the blade severed the rope, which fell onto his legs, and he started to bring his hands around in front of him.

At that instant there was the click of a gun hammer and something touched the back of his head.

"Nice try, Trailsman, but you lose. Do you have any last words?"

10

Skye Fargo went rigid, his arms lowered at his sides, the knife clasped in his right hand but totally useless since he'd get a bullet through the brain if he twitched a single muscle. The gun barrel gouged into his head, forcing him to bow his chin.

"Toss that pigsticker I saw you using," Cutler directed.

Fargo gave a flip of his wrist, and the toothpick sailed a few feet away. "Now what?"

"Now I do what I should have done the first time I laid eyes on you. I knew you were trouble, but Traute wouldn't listen. There's no taming a man like you," Cutler said, backing up. "On your feet. I want you to see it coming."

Putting his hands down, Fargo shoved to his feet. As he rose, he tore a handful of grass loose and held it in his right palm. The mountain man was five feet away. Somehow he must lure Cutler closer. "Where's Shirley?" he asked.

"Out to the world. I gave her a sock on the jaw so she wouldn't traipse off while I was hunting you. She'll be fine once she comes around."

"Until you reach Serenity."

"We all have to meet our Maker sooner or later." Cutler's voice dropped. "My family did. They were butchered like animals, their bodies mutilated, their scalps taken. My wife was raped—" He stopped, unable to continue.

Fargo prepared to hurl himself at Cutler. He had tried his best and lost out, but he wouldn't die like a cow at the slaughter. He wouldn't go down without a struggle. There was always the chance the rifle shot would miss a vital organ. His knees were bending slightly for his spring when he spied movement over Cutler's right shoulder and saw a familiar black-and-white shape moving toward them. The selfsame second his eyes fell on the Ovaro, which was fifteen yards off and had not yet given its presence away, a twig snapped under one of the pinto's hoofs.

Absorbed in thoughts about his family, Jeff Cutler was unaware of the stallion's presence until the crack of the twig. Instinctively he shifted and swung the rifle partway around, and in doing so left his right side unprotected.

In a flash Fargo pounced, covering the space in a single bound, his arms outstretched so that as he closed he threw them wide around Cutler's chest and bore both of them to the earth. Cutler hissed and tried to ram the rifle stock against Fargo's ribs, but Fargo's encircling arms hindered him. Suddenly Cutler whipped his head into Fargo's chin.

Momentarily dazed, Fargo's arms slackened enough for Cutler to break free, rise to his knees, and bring the rifle to bear. Before the barrel was level, Fargo recovered enough to throw himself wildly at Cutler, bowling him over. Cutler sprawled onto his back, the rifle slanted upward, and with a swift kick Fargo sent the gun flying into nearby weeds.

Fargo took a half stride, his fists balled to catch Cutler as he rose, but Cutler was one step ahead of him. Out of nowhere streaked Cutler's right hand, and in it was a long hunting knife. The dully glinting blade swept at Fargo's stomach, missing by a hair.

Rapidly backpedaling and circling, Fargo sought an opening. His own knife was somewhere behind him, but he dared not take his eyes off Cutler to seek it. The mountain man lunged upward and stabbed. This time Fargo felt the blade scrape against the fringe on his buckskin shirt as he dodged aside.

Now the grim fight became a deadly silent battle of animal reflexes, with Cutler thrusting and stabbing again and again and Fargo narrowly evading the blade. They moved in a circle, neither man able to gain the upper hand, as equally matched as it was humanly possible for two men to be.

Fargo tried a feint and nearly lost an eye. He sucked in his gut as the knife arced at his abdomen, then landed a fist to the face that caused Cutler to growl like an enraged bear and move a few inches back. Dropping into a crouch, Fargo moved to his right, wishing he could check the ground for obstacles because a single misstep would mean death.

Sneering wickedly, Cutler suddenly shifted the hunting knife from his right to his left hand, then back again.

It was an old trick designed to keep a foe off balance. A seasoned knife fighter knew to glue his gaze to the knife, not the man holding it, which is what Fargo did, watching the blade pass from hand to hand, waiting for the split second when Cutler's arm would sweep toward his heart or his throat.

He didn't have long to wait.

Cutler speared the knife up and in. The target was Fargo's throat, but Fargo was a shade swifter, sliding to the left out of reach. His chin was fanned by the blade. Lunging, he tried to grasp Cutler's wrist and missed. Cutler countered with a stab that pricked Fargo's forearm. Skipping to the rear so as not to receive a graver wound, Fargo felt his left boot heel catch on something. Suddenly he fell.

Cutler took instant advantage, raising his hunting knife on high for a downward plunge as he sprang for the kill.

Flat on his back, his arms outflung, seemingly as defenseless as a newborn fawn, Fargo proved that his reputation was well earned by driving both legs upward, his boots striking Cutler in the stomach. Cutler was catapulted back to the dank soil, landing with a thud. Fargo heaved erect and reached Cutler before he could stand, clamping his hand on Cutler's knife arm while his fist slammed into Cutler's jaw. That punch would have stunned most men, but Cutler seemed to be made of iron; he snarled and tried to tear his arm free.

For seconds they struggled, neither man with an edge. Then Fargo slammed his knee into Cutler's exposed elbow, and Cutler involuntarily cried out in pain. A second blow numbed Cutler's hand. The knife fell from his limp fingers onto the ground between them.

Cutler, enraged, got his good arm around Fargo's legs and pulled. Fargo tried to resist, but they toppled together, Cutler winding up on top. He seized hold of Fargo's neck with both hands although his right one was still weak, his thumbs digging in deep.

Clutching Cutler's wrists, Fargo attempted to pry the man's hands from his throat. Cutler's strength was incredible. Straining with all the might he could muster, Fargo barely budged the fingers constricting tighter and tighter. He began to have difficulty breathing. Thrashing violently, he succeeded in turning them onto their sides. His right fist crashed into Cutler's cheek but had no effect. Reaching out with his left hand to try and shove Cutler away, his fingers brushed a hard object on the ground.

Jeff Cutler's face was contorted in a maniacal mask of sheer hatred, his eyes alight with bloodthirsty delight. He laughed as he sought to strangle the life from the man who had reminded him of his unending torment. He laughed until the cold steel lanced into his chest.

Fargo held the knife steady, the blade buried to the hilt, and felt Cutler stiffen. He expected Cutler to put up a tremendous fight to the last. Instead, Cutler's grip broke, his hands fell, his body sagged, and he rolled onto his back. Pushing to his knees, Fargo whipped the knife above his head for another blow. None was needed.

Great ragged breaths fluttered from Cutler's parted lips. He gurgled, then looked at Fargo. His hand rose limply but plopped onto the grass. Feebly, he struggled to speak, the words rasping from his throat. "Knew . . . come to this . . . one day."

"It didn't have to," Fargo said. "You made the choice."

Cutler licked his lips, said. "Had to. Miss them so damn much."

Fargo stared down at the dying mountain man, his fists clenched.

"You're good . . . Trailsman."

Fargo said nothing.

"Thank you," Cutler whispered and tried to say more but couldn't. His eyes flared, his nostrils quivered, and his chin pointed at the heavens. Exhaling loudly, he became still.

There were soft footfalls to the west, and Fargo glanced up to find Shirley walking toward them.

"Is he dead?"

"Yes."

"Thank God! You think you know some people, and they turn on you like that. Good riddance, I say."

"Shirley?"

"What, lover?"

"Shut up." Fargo placed the hunting knife on Cutler's chest, then scoured the grass until he found his Arkansas toothpick and slid it into the sheath inside his boot. Adjusting his pant leg, he straightened.

"I don't understand. Why are you mad at me? What did I do?" Shirley asked.

Rather than get into a long explanation, Fargo changed the subject. "He told me that he knocked you out."

"He damn near did," Shirley said, smiling tentatively and touching a hand to her chin. "Hit me hard enough to break a brick, but I've been punched by the best of 'em. Some of the men I've been with have had the dispositions of wolverines. Say one wrong word and they tear into you with both fists flying." She glanced at Cutler. "He hit me and I played possum until he left."

"Smart girl," Fargo said, grinning when she did. Taking her hand, he went to the Ovaro, mounted, and conducted a search until he recovered both her horse and Cutler's. His guns were tied in the bedroll on Cutler's dun. In no time he had the Colt on his hip and the Sharps snug in his saddle scabbard.

"So now what?" Shirley inquired, watching him.

"We find a spot for you to lay up for a spell while I pay Traute a visit."

"Can't we just light a shuck for Denver?"

"You know better. We've already been through this."

"But there's nothing that says I have to like it."

With her following on the mare and him leading the fine dun, Fargo rode in the same direction they had been going before he tried his risky gambit. Shirley cleared her throat, and he knew what was coming.

"Aren't you going the wrong way?"

"Nope."

"But you're taking me back toward Serenity. I thought you wanted to get me off in the woods somewhere so I'll be safe?"

"Changed my mind," Fargo said.

"That's supposed to be a woman's prerogative. Mind telling my why? If I'm about to die, I'd at least like to know the reason. Your brainstorm should be downright educational."

Women! Fargo reflected wryly. They had sarcasm down to a science. If it wasn't for their sensual charms and the fun-loving company they could be when they were in the right mood, men would prefer to sleep alone. "I first wanted to get you as far from the valley as I could because I knew Traute would send someone after us. Now that I know he sent only Cutler, I can take you back to the wagon trail that Traute uses to transport his silver to Denver or wherever else. This way, if something happens to me, you have a fair chance of making it back on your own."

"Why, Skye," Shirley said lightly. "I do believe those are the most words you've thrown my way since we hooked up. Did you wear your gums out talking that much?" She tossed her head and laughed.

"*You're* in fine spirits."

"I should say so. You just pulled my fat out of the fire and I'm glad to be alive."

"That's nice."

Shirley clucked her mare up alongside the pinto and reached out to trace a finger along his outer thigh. "Real glad, if you get my meaning."

"Not now."

"Then how about when we stop?"

"I have other things on my mind."

"And you men have the gall to claim women are contrary! When men want a tumble in the sack, we have to drop everything to oblige them. But when women get romantic notions, men act like they can't be bothered. The whole bunch of you are as thick-headed as mules."

That worked both ways, Fargo thought to himself, prudently holding his tongue. She scowled at him, then fell into place behind the dun. An hour went by. Two. He realized they wouldn't reach the spot he wanted until the wee hours of the morning, and they were already bushed. So at the next clearing he drew reins and announced, "We'll make camp here for the night."

"You sly devil," Shirley said and giggled.

Fargo didn't like the sound of that. He needed plenty of rest if he was to confront Vincent Traute the next day. While Shirley busied herself behind a convenient bush, he tended to their animals, stripping off the saddles and giving each horse a hasty rubdown. Taking two blankets, he arranged them on the grass and gratefully sank onto his back. It felt so good to rest! he thought, aligning the brim of his hat over his eyes. Putting both hands under his head, he smiled and waited to drift off.

She approached so quietly he didn't realize she was there until her warm fingers touched his neck and her yielding lips pecked him on the cheek.

"Not now," he growled.

"There's no need to play hard to get. I know you want me."

"I want to sleep."

"Secretly you don't. Secretly you can't wait to ravish me."

"Where *do* you get your crazy notions?" Fargo said, his last word smothered by her descending mouth. He felt her lips flush with his, felt her silken tongue contact his own, and he reluctantly responded. When she finally broke for air, he settled down again and said, "Satisfied?"

"Not by a long shot."

Fargo heard clothing rustle. She gripped his right hand, raising it, and suddenly his palm closed on her naked breast. Opening his eyes, he found himself eyeball to nipple with her other full globe. "Damn. Don't you know how to take no for an answer?"

Smiling seductively, Shirley lowered her free breast, allowing the hard nipple to brush his mouth. "Don't fight it. Secretly you want me."

"Secretly I'd like to tan your backside."

Her smile became positively wicked. "Be my guest. I like it rough now and then."

Fargo's mind was telling him to push her away and sleep, but his body turned traitor. Before he could stop himself, he had sucked the nipple into his mouth and was tweaking it with his tongue.

"Ohhhh, yes! I knew you were hungry, and I don't mean for food."

Had his hands been free, Fargo might have gagged her. But his traitorous fingers were kneading her breasts as if they were pliant dough. His mouth, meanwhile, gave her nipple the royal treatment.

"Mmmmm. Nice," Shirley said, running her fingers

111

through his hair. "You have a way about you. But I guess I've already told you that." She sat astraddle him, her hips over his middle, her long hair cascading onto his upturned face. "Keep this up and I promise you won't regret it."

Fargo was already regretting it. In the back of his mind he cursed himself for being the dunderhead of all time. When he should be sleeping, when he should be saving his energy for the life-and-death struggle awaiting him in Serenity, here he was indulging in his favorite pastime. One day, he reflected, a woman would be the death of him.

He devoted his attention to her breasts for the better part of ten minutes, making them slick, soft, and hot. Her left hand had fallen from his hair, and when he glanced down at her waist he saw it was under her skirt, tending to the preliminaries. "I'll handle that," he growled, pulling her hand out and replacing it with his own. She gasped as his fingers touched her slit.

"I want you so much, handsome. You have no idea."

"Trust me. I do." She pressed a breast against him and he drew it into his mouth. Under her his manhood twitched, firmed, and surged, becoming a steely pole.

"Any time," she purred.

With a jerk, Fargo flipped her onto her back, reversing their positions. "You want it rough," he said, "you'll get it rough."

"Promises, promises."

He ground himself into her, rubbing her nether mound with his organ through the buckskin and dress material separating their skin, and she squirmed deliciously. Taking hold of her breasts, he squeezed until they were ripe to burst. She cooed in ecstasy, her bottom rising to meet hips. Then he kissed her, but not lightly as before. This time he kissed her with unbridled passion, his lips mashing hers, his thumbs rooted to her nipples. She met his ardor with equal ardor, all lava and lace.

Her smooth neck enticed his tongue, then her ears. Normally he didn't waste much time on earlobes, but now he did, savoring each one as if it was candy, sucking until they swelled. She had dabbed strong perfume behind her ears the morning they left Serenity, and the tantalizing fragrance lingered, reminding him of the scent of lilacs after a spring shower.

She was busy, meanwhile, lathering his throat and pulling back his shirt so she could bite his broad shoulders. Her hands roamed everywhere, her nails biting into his flesh. Tiny moans wafted from her rosy lips.

When Fargo drew back from her ears, he gripped her hair on both sides and twisted her head, offering her lips more fully to his. Their kiss ignited a spark that rippled down both their bodies. Her thighs were fitted to his, and he could feel her inner heat warming his organ.

Again he swooped to her swelling breasts, bringing them to the peak of heaving excitement.

"Damn, you're the best!" Shirley breathed. "I wish more men knew your secret."

Fargo stopped and looked up, his eyes twinkling. "How'd you know?" he responded.

"Know what?" she asked, puzzled.

"That I have a secret."

"You do? I was only joking. Tell me."

"I learned it from an old Sioux who'd taken four wives," he said, undoing more of her dress.

"The horny bastard. What did he say?"

Purposely, Fargo rimmed her belly button with the tip of his tongue, stalling to heighten the suspense.

"Tell me, blast you!" she declared, giving his arm a whack with her palm.

"You wouldn't understand," he teased.

"You son of a bitch. I know all there is to know about sex. I practically invented it." Shirley paused and grabbed his red bandanna. "So tell me!"

By then Fargo had both hands right where he wanted them, at the edge of her bunched dress. "No," he said, and smirked. "We'll talk later." No sooner were the words out of his mouth than Fargo inserted his fingers, using them to drive her over the brink of self-control. She groaned and heaved. She uttered little cries and thrust against him. She sobbed once or twice from the intensity of her arousal. There had never been a woman more ready than she was when Fargo entered her.

Her nails sank into his biceps. She bit his chin, his cheek, the side of his neck.

"Oh! Oh! Oh!"

Fargo held himself in check, admiring her earthy beauty, waiting until she spent and her trembling subsided. Then he began stroking, pushing in deep, over and over. Her eyes became limpid pools of lust, fixed on his.

"I'm just getting warmed up," Fargo promised, grasping her hips to aid his penetration. The friction of her inner walls on his manhood was exquisite. He kissed her and swore her lips were hot enough to burn skin. Slowly the tension in his loins grew more and more, and when he could no longer stand it, when she was begging him to give her his all, he pounded like a madman and gushed like a geyser.

Shirley found her voice, the forest echoing to her scream. "Aaeeiii! Yes, big man! Yes, that's it!"

11

By ten o'clock the next morning Skye Fargo was riding alone toward the outlaw-infested town of Serenity. Several miles behind him Shirley, the mare, and the dun were well concealed in a stand of aspens close to a ribbon of a creek. She had given him a particularly passionate kiss before he rode off and told him to watch his back, the look in her eyes revealing she truly cared.

Fargo shifted in the saddle to relieve the discomfort below his belt. They had made love twice as if each time would be their last, and neither of them had fallen asleep until almost morning. As he had feared, he was tired and sore, not at his best as he should be if he planned to tangle with the cutthroats ruling the isolated valley.

He held the Sharps across his thighs, a cartridge in the chamber, his thumb resting close to the hammer. In his holster nestled the Colt, in his boot his knife. Wrapped in his bedroll was the shotgun he'd taken from the marshal's office. He'd left Cutler's rifle and plenty of ammunition with Shirley.

Fargo half expected to find guards posted at the gorge, but there were none. Evidently Traute had enough confidence in Cutler not to worry, which was Traute's mistake. Fargo was going to give him plenty to worry about.

All told, he figured that he was up against about a dozen guns. Certainly not much more than that. Of them all the only one reputed to be exceptionally fast was Ringald. But twelve-to-one odds weren't to be taken lightly. He must wage a war of attrition, wear them down little by little, rather than ride right up to the ranch or straight into town and be blown to pieces before he could hope to kill the brains behind the vile operation.

Fargo smiled in anticipation as he contemplated his strategy. There were three points for him to focus on.

The first was the mine, where the prisoners who were still alive were suffering the torments of the damned daily. They must be freed and taken out of harm's way before he did anything else.

Then there was the so-called ranch on the south side of the valley, which according to Shirley consisted of three buildings. There was a long, low sod-and-log structure close to the mountains. Nearby was a barn used to store feed for the livestock. Behind the house, and guarded day and night, sat a large shed where Traute stored his silver ore. Shirley had explained that the ore was freighted to Denver along a trail that paralleled the other trail Fargo had first followed into the valley for a few miles. Then it branched eastward to follow flatter, more open terrain to the southeast.

Last on his list was Serenity itself, the vipers' den. The town was the clever lure that drew in the unsuspecting, innocent wanderers who became Traute's virtual slaves. It wouldn't do to wipe out the outlaws and leave the town alone since another batch of vermin might breed in the same place. No, he had a special fate in store for Serenity.

Once through the gorge Fargo galloped to the nearest cover, the trees, and worked his way along the north border of the valley where the woods were thickest. He lost sight of the road but every so often glimpsed the town through breaks in the pines. By midafternoon he was exactly where he wanted to be, at the base of the mountain containing the mine.

Reining up in a clearing, Fargo slid down, ground-hitched the pinto so it could graze, and sat with his back to a trunk. All that riding had left him drowsy. Since he needed rest anyway, and since he was confident he would awaken once the sun sank below the horizon and the temperature dropped dramatically, as it invariably did at upper elevations, he soon dozed off.

A cool northwesterly breeze brought him back to life an hour after the sun set. Standing, he stretched and scanned the slope of the mountain. Pinpoints of light identified where the shack and cabin stood, and mounting, he rode toward them. The Sharps went into its scabbard so he could pull out the shotgun. At close range there was nothing like buckshot for filling a man with lead, which was why more and more lawmen were relying on shotguns for town use.

By now, he reflected, the prisoners would be in the cabin, finishing off their miserable meal. The guards should be in the shack. He swung around so as to come up on the shack from the rear, and when he was close enough to see it, he dismounted, tied the pinto to a tree, and advanced stealthily, cocking the shotgun first. Gruff laughter issued from the sole window. The guards, at least, were enjoying themselves.

At the corner he paused, listening. From the voices he deduced there were only two men inside, just as before, and the tinkle of a fork or a spoon onto a tin plate told him they were eating their supper. Creeping to the front corner, he peeked at the door, which hung open five or six inches, then at two horses tethered to his right. One was chomping on grass, the other watching him as if unsure whether he was friend or foe. Hoping the animal wouldn't whinny, he slowly edged around the corner to the door jamb.

"—wait for Cutler to fetch them back," someone was saying. "The boss says we can all have her as long as we want for free. I bet you I plumb wear my dingus out!"

"We'll kill her with love," the second man said, and they both laughed uproariously.

They were still laughing when Fargo stepped into the doorway and leveled the double-barreled shotgun. "Howdy, boys," he said softly. "What was that I just heard about someone dying?"

For several seconds they were transfixed by the sight of the hawk-eyed harbinger of vengeance framed in their doorway, then they both vented oaths and galvanized into motion, clawing for their pistols. The first blast caught the faster of the pair in the face and blew his head apart, while the second man was hit in the neck and nearly decapitated. They toppled one after the other, taking their chairs with them.

The key to the shackles had been replaced on the hook. Fargo quickly grabbed it and hastened to the cabin where he hurled the door wide and entered. There they were, gaping in amazement, Rice, Yost, and Carson, the latter's left shoulder covered with a bloodstained bandage.

"You!" Rice declared, coming to his feet. "They didn't kill you after all! Traute said they had."

"I don't die that easy," Fargo said, moving to Carson first and kneeling to undo the man's shackle.

"You came back!" the young man said, his eyes watering. "You were free and clear, but you came back for us."

"How bad off are you?" Fargo asked, nodding at the wound. "Can you ride?"

"If it means finally escaping from this hellhole, just watch me," Carson replied. He touched the bandage, which had been crudely made out of strips from an old, dirty shirt, and frowned. "I'm not going to let a little thing like a gunshot stop me now."

"They tossed Haggerty in a shallow hole," Yost said. "Stripped off his clothes and just dumped him in." He bowed his head. "I wish I'd had a gun in my hands. That old man was like a second pa to all of us."

Swiftly Fargo went from prisoner to prisoner and freed all three; then they hurried out to the horses. Carson swung up behind Rice, Yost took the other animal, and Fargo led them to where he had left the Ovaro.

"Where now?" Rice asked.

"I'm getting you out of here," Fargo said, wedging the shotgun into his bedroll. He climbed up, turned to the north, and brought the stallion to a trot. On the valley floor Serenity was no more than a series of lights against an inky backdrop. From that high up it was impossible to distinguish the buildings. So far there did not appear to be any uproar in the town as there would be if the shotgun blasts had been heard. But now the wind was blowing up-slope instead of down-slope, and Fargo doubted the noise had carried that far.

Once at the bottom they made much better time. Fargo had only to go over a route once, and from then on he knew it. He had an uncanny knack for remembering landmarks and reading the lay of the land like most men read books. Their ride to the gorge proved uneventful. On the other end they broke into a gallop.

"That was easier than I figured it would be," Rice commented.

"Don't get your hopes up yet. Traute is bound to send

Cutler after us come first light, and they say that man can track anyone anywhere. He'll find us."

"No, he won't," Fargo said.

"How can you be certain?" Carson asked.

"Because he already found me."

"Oh. Mr. Fargo, I'm beginning to get the idea that you're not a man to trifle with."

"Tell that to Traute."

When still fifty yards from the stand where Shirley waited, Fargo cupped a hand to his mouth and called out, "Don't shoot, woman! We're on your side."

"Who are you talking to?" Rice inquired.

"You'll see."

She came into the open to greet them, the rifle in the crook of her arm. "Well, I declare! It's nice to see you boys again. For a minute there I thought Traute had caught Fargo and persuaded him to tell where I was and those murdering polecats were coming after me."

"Is that coffee I smell?" Rice asked.

Shirley nodded and grinned. "Courtesy of Mr. Jeff Cutler, who has no further use for it. God rest his soul." She motioned for them to dismount. "Come on. There's plenty for everyone but we'll have to share cups."

"Not me," Fargo said, turning the pinto. "I have more work to do."

"Tonight? Can't it wait until morning?"

"No," Fargo said. He jerked his thumb at the aspens. "I want all of you to stay put until I get back. Don't stir away from these trees for anything. You have enough water and jerky to last two days, and I should return well before you run out."

"What are you up to next?" Shirley inquired. "You've already ruined Traute's mining operation."

"I'm just starting."

She came over and placed a hand on his leg. "Do me a favor, Skye."

"If I can."

"Don't hurt Gloria. She's a friend."

"She had her chance to come with us."

"I know. Don't hold it against her, though. She never has been the brightest filly in the pasture. She sees Traute as the top bull so she won't buck him. If you can

119

make her see the light, she'll come around to our way of thinking. I guarantee she will."

"I'll see what I can do," Fargo said, "but I'm not making any promises."

"Thanks, handsome," Shirley said, giving his arm a squeeze. "I'll be in your debt," she added softly, turning so the others couldn't see and brazenly rubbing her breasts against his leg.

"Don't you *ever* get enough?"

"Honey, the day I get enough is the day they plant me in my grave. Life is too short. We have to take the good things it has to offer when they come along or we'll miss them."

"Keep that notion until I return," Fargo said, putting his heels to the stallion's flanks. He had a lot of ground to cover before dawn and couldn't afford to waste any time. Reentering the gorge, he cut to the south, staying within stone-throwing distance of the base of the mountains. Eventually, he knew, his course would bring him to Traute's ranch.

Only an hour of night remained when Fargo spied the buildings. His urgency proved well founded. Already someone was up, fixing breakfast, and gray smoke curled from a stone chimney. There were nine horses in a corral attached to the barn and a wagon parked near the shed. He moved as close as he dared, swung down, and crept to the edge of the trees.

Western folk were notoriously early risers. In addition to whoever was cooking their meal and two guards in front of the ore shack, there was a man in the barn forking hay from a loft.

Fargo made himself comfortable. Before he could move against Traute he must learn exactly how many outlaws were at the ranch and study their work routine so he would know when they were most vulnerable.

By sunrise seven more men had filed from the living quarters to avail themselves of the outhouse. They washed up using a basin on the front porch. Afterward they all went in to eat, and forty-five minutes later the ranch buzzed with activity. Two men worked at saddling the horses while another drove the wagon right up to the front of the shed. Minutes later Vincent Traute himself strolled out into the brightening sunlight, five hardcases on his heels. They walked to the shed, where Traute removed a large padlock and chain, and presently they were loading ore into the wagon bed.

Fargo's interest perked up. Could it be the outlaws were planning to deliver a load to the man who bought from them in Denver? He watched them fill the bed, then cover it with heavy canvas which they securely tied down. By then six of the horses had been saddled.

Traute mounted a bay and barked orders. Provisions were brought from the house to be piled behind the driver's seat. Five other hardcases swung onto their horses, and within minutes the whole procession was moving toward the trail to the gorge, the riders in the lead.

Sliding backward until he could safely stand, Fargo jogged to the stallion. Here was an unexpected development he could use to his advantage. He wanted to make Traute pay through the nose for all the suffering the man had caused, and what better way than to put a dent in Traute's bankroll?

Keeping the slow moving wagon in sight was ridiculously easy. Fargo kept well in the shadows so as not to be discovered, and he couldn't help but note that Traute's band acted as if they didn't have a care in the world—they joked, laughed, and generally treated the trip as a lark. So many years of doing as they damn well pleased had made them complacent and careless. Which suited Fargo just fine.

He thought about the ore in that wagon. The silver vein had to be an especially rich one to justify the trouble of taking such heavy loads to Denver and the cost of refining the ore to obtain the precious metal. From what Haggerty had revealed, the mine produced what was known as compound ore, silver joined to sulfur, which required smelting to free the metal from the compound. Given the current market value of silver, he guessed that Traute made three or four thousand dollars on each trip. In itself that wasn't much, but if Traute made fifteen to twenty trips a year, then the mine was bringing in forty-five thousand dollars or more annually. And how long did Haggerty say Traute had been doing this? Ten years or better? Vincent Traute was slowly but surely accumulating an incredible fortune.

Fargo wondered about something else: Where did

Traute keep his money? The outlaw might deposit the funds in a bank, but Fargo doubted it. Traute was the kind to want the money stashed close by where he could rub his greedy fingers through his hoard whenever the whim struck him. Fargo speculated on whether the ill-gotten gains might be hidden somewhere at the ranch. It was an idea worth filing away for future consideration.

The clattering wagon and the high-spirited outlaws made their way to the gorge and disappeared within its high rock walls.

As Fargo watched them talking and grinning like so many school kids out on a field trip, it occurred to him they were going to Denver—the big city with its lively brothels, smoke-filled gambling dens, and a thousand other voices in which they could wildly indulge to their heart's content. After being cooped up in the valley for weeks at a stretch, their only sources of entertainment the dull saloon and the same two women in Serenity, they must be bursting at the seams, anxious to guzzle their fill at the trough of human pleasure.

To give them time to pass on through the gorge, Fargo dallied for several minutes. He knew the wagon trail would take the outlaws within a hundred yards of the aspens where Shirley and the freed prisoners were concealed, and he hoped they would do nothing to give themselves away. Thinking of Shirley brought a smile to his lips. She certainly was a handful. If all went well, maybe he'd treat her to a fancy meal in Denver after he had settled matters with Traute. Then they could hole up in a hotel room for a day or two to see which one of them wore out first.

Satisfied the outlaws had been given enough time, Fargo entered the gorge and cautiously made his way to the far side. He stopped shy of the opening and leaned forward, craning his neck until he could see the wagon raising swirls of dust as it rumbled eastward.

He had to stay there until they went around a curve and were hidden by trees. Deciding that he shouldn't leave anything to chance, he galloped into the open, bearing to the left, and plunged into another stretch of forest. From there he swung wide past the outlaws, who could go no faster than the overburdened wagon, and soon reached the aspens. At the very center he found the four of them huddled around a small fire.

Rice now had Cutler's rifle, and along with the others he jumped up as the pinto plowed through the slender trees, tucking the stock to his shoulder. When he recognized Fargo, he promptly lowered the gun. "Damn! You gave me a fright. I was afraid Traute had found us."

"What are you doing here so soon?" Shirley asked. "You made it sound as if we wouldn't see you for a couple of days."

"You're about to have company," Fargo warned. "Traute is on his way out with another ore shipment, and he'll pass by here in under ten minutes."

"Should we move?" Carson asked. He appeared peaked and was holding his wounded shoulder with his good hand.

"No need," Fargo said. "Just keep low and have someone keep an eye on the horses to stop them from whinnying." The fire, which gave off wispy tendrils of smoke, was no problem since the tendrils were dissipated by the branches above.

"I'll handle the horses," Yost volunteered.

Fargo swung down and tied the stallion to a tree. As he turned, a steaming cup of coffee was pushed at his face.

"Here, handsome. Why not wet your whistle while you have a minute? And maybe you'll see fit to tell us what you have in mind."

"Thanks," Fargo said, taking the proffered cup and sipping the refreshing brew. He smacked his lips as the coffee warmed his innards, then he crouched by the fire and held his hands close to the tiny flames. All eyes, he noticed, were on him. Somehow, he got the feeling they had been doing some serious talking about their situation right before he showed up.

"Yeah," Rice threw in. "What are your plans, if you don't object to letting us know?"

"My plans aren't written in stone. I'm playing this by ear, doing what I can when I can. Why?"

Rice shrugged, then glanced at Shirley.

"We've been giving it some thought," she said, "and

we're not too sure staying put like this is a good idea. I mean, there are four of us now, and we have three horses. We think we can make it to Denver with a little luck."

"Yost is a fair hand at finding his way by the sun and the stars," Rice mentioned quickly. "He can make certain that we stay on the right track." Rather nervously he nodded at Carson. "And you can see for yourself that George is getting worse. Infection is trying to set in. He needs a doc and he needs one pronto."

"You're all agreed?" Fargo asked.

"We haven't put it to a vote, but we all feel the same way," Shirley said. She stepped up to him and crouched at his side. "Sorry, lover, but I'm not one for outdoor living. I like warm baths every day and smooth sheets at night. I like to look in a mirror when I do my hair. And I like smelling as sweet as a rose, not like a day-old sock."

"You smell fine to me."

Her eyes crinkled. "To a man who spends most of his time in the company of a horse, any women smells good." She draped a hand on his arm. "What do you think? Should we try to reach Denver or wait until you're ready to take us? I should tell you we really want to go, but we'll abide by whatever you say."

"I'm not forcing any of you to stay," Fargo said. "If you feel you can do it, go right ahead."

"We'll talk it over some more, then make up our minds," Shirley said. She pecked him on the cheek. "If it was just up to me, I'd probably wait for you to give the word, baths or no baths. But young Carson, there, won't last the week out if that gunshot becomes more infected."

"Has it been cauterized?"

It was Rice who answered. "Twice. We cauterized a second time when we saw that the shoulder was swelling terribly. Not that it did much good. I lanced the wound earlier, and you wouldn't believe all the pus that came out."

Carson had sagged to the ground and was sitting doubled over, his hand still on his arm. When he looked at Fargo his features betrayed his pain. "Sorry, Trailsman. I guess we all can't be as tough as you."

"It could happen to anyone," Fargo said, reaching across to press his hand to Carson's brow. The skin was hot enough to fry eggs. "You take it easy. We won't let you die."

Just then Yost hissed a warning at them. "Pssssst! Quiet! Here come those rotten killers!"

12

Skye Fargo knelt at the edge of the aspens and rested his right hand on his Colt. Nothing had changed where the outlaws were concerned; Traute and the rest were still behaving as if they didn't have a care in the world. Traute seemed to be in the best spirits of all, perhaps because he was keenly looking forward to adding a few thousand dollars to his cached wealth.

"We could pick off two or three of those vultures before they even knew what hit 'em," Rice whispered on Fargo's left.

"And the rest would surround us and keep us pinned down until they sent for more men," Fargo responded. "No, we sit tight until they're gone."

On his other side Shirley asked softly, "Who's that coming up behind them?"

Fargo had already spotted the rider out of the corner of his eye. A shout arose from the man in question, one of Traute's gang riding hell bent for leather to catch up with the wagon. He flailed his straining mount with a short quirt and yelled, "Hold on there! Hold on!"

"What does it mean?" Rice wondered.

A possible answer popped unbidden into Fargo's mind, and he hoped he was wrong. The wagon stopped. Traute moved to meet the newcomer, who drew rein and breathlessly reported, his frantic words inaudible because of the distance. A change came over the expression of every outlaw, a change for the worse, and suddenly Traute was issuing curt orders while gesturing with his hand.

"I know what it must be about!" Rice whispered. "They've finally found out that we've escaped."

"That would be my hunch," Fargo said, wishing Traute would have been long gone before anyone rode up to the mine and found the bodies of the guards. Now what would Traute do? Postpone the trip to Denver? Begin a thorough hunt for the missing prisoners? Fargo didn't have to wait long to find out.

Traute and the man who had brought the bad news raced back toward the gorge while the wagon and the five guards resumed their interrupted journey.

Only when the trail was clear in both directions did Fargo stand and walk to the Ovaro. These new developments threw a whole new light on the affair. Earlier it had all been so simple. He'd planned to trail the wagon and find a convenient spot to put the outlaws afoot. Then he would have given them the chance to lay down their guns so he could turn them over to the law, or else suffer the consequences. They would probably have resisted, which pleased him greatly.

Shirley materialized at his side. "What now?"

A glance showed Carson asleep by the fire, so Fargo could speak plainly. "He needs medicine or he'll never make it halfway to Denver. Is there any in Serenity?"

"Griswald has some at the saloon for when fights break out and such." She gripped his shoulder. "But if you go back in there you're asking for trouble. They'll be as stirred up as a hornet's nest."

"Give me until tonight. If I'm not back by then, figure the worst has happened and do as you want," Fargo said, climbing into the saddle and gripping the reins in his left hand.

"But Griswald might not have anything we can use."

"So we do nothing and just let Carson die?"

That gave her pause. She stared thoughtfully at the slumbering youth for a moment, then turned a contrite look on Fargo. "You're a far better man than most folks give you credit for being."

"Don't let it get around," Fargo said with a wink. He touched his hat and rode from the stand to the trail, where he paused to gaze both ways. The deep ruts left by the wagon were freshly imprinted in the earth. How easy it would be to follow them and prevent the shipment from traveling another mile. But his vengeance must wait. Wheeling the pinto, he rode hard for town.

In the blaze of the afternoon sun Serenity was as lifeless as ever. There wasn't a single horse at any of the hitching posts. Acting on the assumption that all of the remaining outlaws would be up at the mine, Fargo circled around behind the buildings and approached the saloon from the rear. The door was cracked to let in air. He slowly pushed it open, thankful the hinges didn't creak, and drew and cocked the Colt. Working his way forward along a narrow, dark hall, he reached the kitchen. A potbellied stove dominated the room, with stew simmering on top.

Through a doorway beyond Fargo could see the interior of the saloon. Nothing moved; all was quiet. He started across the kitchen, the sight and heady aroma of the slowly bubbling broth causing his stomach to rumble. He hadn't had a decent meal since that morning Shirley fixed him breakfast. Halting, he scooped a spoonful of stew into his mouth, swirled it around on his tongue, and swallowed. If nothing else, Griswald was a fine cook.

In the saloon a glass tinkled.

Fargo was suddenly all business, crouching and gliding to the doorway where he commanded a view of the entire room. Griswald was gone, and all the tables except one were empty. Seated at a corner card table, her hair in disarray, was the other fallen dove, Gloria, a half-empty whiskey bottle before her, a full glass in her hand. As he watched, she took a swig, gulping greedily, then sluggishly wiped the back of her hand across her red lips in a very unladylike fashion, smearing her lipstick.

He moved to his right, behind the bar, making no attempt to hide. She was staring morosely out the front window, lost in an inner world of her own. As he walked around the end of the bar, he saw an empty bottle on the floor at her feet and marveled that she wasn't passed out under the table.

"Where's Griswald?" he asked softly.

Gloria reacted as if prodded with a pitchfork, nearly jumping out of her chair and spilling the rotgut onto her dress. She gaped at him in horror, her mouth working soundlessly before she blurted, "You! It's really you."

The woman was a mess. She had been crying earlier, and there were smudge marks down both cheeks and black smears under both of her eyes, which were bloodshot and watery. Her fingers, when she raised a hand to point at him, trembled uncontrollably. "You have your nerve, damn you! Coming back here after you took her away."

Fargo glanced at the front entrance. "You had your chance to go with us."

"Shirley was the best friend I ever had and you sweet-talked her into throwing her life away. You should be strung up by the thumbs and have your jewels hacked off."

"Where's Griswald?" Fargo repeated.

"How the hell should I know? Do you think they bother to tell me every time one of them goes to take a leak?" She brushed awkwardly at her hair and tried to sit up straight. "He went out when there was a lot of yelling in the street, and he ain't been back yet."

"Did you see Traute?"

"No, but I heard him. He's a regular grizzly when he's mad, and he was as mad as could be." Her eyes narrowed. "I'll bet you had something to do with that, didn't you?"

"Is anyone else left in town besides you?"

Gloria sat back, swaying slightly, and pounded her right fist on the table. "Why do you keep asking me all these stupid questions? What do I look like, the town crier?" She tittered, then burst into a raucous cackle. "The town crier! Ain't I a card!"

Ignoring her, Fargo went to the bat-wing doors and checked the street. Not so much as an insect moved. Either Griswald was in one of the other buildings or the bartender had gone off with Traute. Maybe Traute had pressed every man in the valley into joining the hunt.

"I've changed my mind," Gloria announced.

"What?" Fargo said absently while staring in the direction of the ranch. If no one was there, he mused, now would be the ideal time for him to nose around and see if he could find Traute's hoard. Perhaps he should swing by on his way back with the medicine. But could Carson hold out that long?

"I've changed my mind," Gloria reiterated. "Take me, too."

He glanced at her in annoyance, bothered by her drunken chatter. "Take you where?"

"Where else, dunderhead? I want you to take me to wherever you took Shirley."

"Now?"

"Right this minute. I won't even bother to pack. Just get me out of here before Traute comes back."

Fargo recalled his promise to Shirley and reluctantly nodded. With Gloria along the notion of paying the ranch house a visit was out of the question. In her sodden state she would slow him down too much. Sighing, he walked to the table. For Carson's sake he must head straight for the aspens and ride to the ranch later. "Do you have a horse?"

"Not one of my own. But there's a whole bunch down at the livery." She stood unsteadily and put a hand on the table for support. "We'll take one of those. Old Vince won't miss one measly little critter. And if he does, screw him!"

"First we need medicine," Fargo said, heading for the bar. Behind it were shelves filled with bottles, glasses, dishes, and sundry odds and ends typical of any saloon. There were a few boxes, and he checked in each one. A belch at the counter made him turn.

"What do you need medicine for?" Gloria inquired, slurring her words badly.

"Carson is bad off. Shirley told me that Griswald keeps some handy."

"Yep," Gloria said, nodding vigorously. Her eyes narrowed as she intently scanned the shelves. "Look for a leather pouch. He won it in a poker game at a trading post years ago and keeps the stuff in there."

It took five minutes to find. The old beaded pouch, which at one time must have belonged to a Crow Indian, was in a corner at the back of the lower shelf. He opened the flap and inspected the contents; castor oil, Epsom salts, tinctures, and, much to his surprise, laudanum. "This will do nicely," he said.

"Can we take a bottle along, too, in case I get thirsty?"

"No."

Gloria pouted. "I don't understand what Shirley sees in you. You're no fun."

He grabbed her wrist and roughly hauled her around the end of the bar, then through the kitchen to the back door where he paused to survey the dark mountain housing the mine and to see if there was anyone lurking at the back of the buildings. The coast appeared clear.

"What's your rush?" Gloria asked testily, trying to pull her wrist loose. "You keep on like this and you'll make me sick."

"You shouldn't drink so much if you can't hold your liquor."

She giggled like a schoolgirl. "If you only knew, lover! If you only knew!"

Half regretting his promise to Shirley, Fargo moved to the Ovaro, grabbed the reins, and hurried the length of the town until he reached the rear door to the barn. It was closed. Motioning for Gloria to stay there, he held the Colt at waist level and went in. Only two stalls contained horses, and there wasn't a living soul on the premises.

It took less than two minutes to saddle one of the mounts and lead it out. Gloria gripped the saddle horn and swung on board without being told. "Ready when you are, grumpy."

Rather than swing wide to the south or north and take a full hour longer in getting back, Fargo went around the corner of the livery at a gallop and flew to the east. He repeatedly looked at the fronts of the buildings, expecting to see the telltale gleam of sunlight on a gun barrel, but no one tried to stop them. Once again he had been lucky. Or so he thought.

The ride went surprisingly well. Gloria sat in the saddle as if born to it and never once swayed, had a foot slip out of the stirrups, or committed any of the mistakes inebriated riders usually did. Neither did she babble on about sheer nonsense as some drunks would do. Not until they reached the gorge did she speak.

"How much farther?"

"Not far. You'll see," Fargo answered, gazing up at the towering walls. He was puzzled by Traute's failure to post guards at the gorge. For a thorough man who usually thought of everything, Traute was strangely negligent at times.

Rice saw them approaching and stepped from the aspens, smiling broadly, the rifle cradled in his arms. "Howdy, Gloria! Glad to see you've come to your senses. Shirley will be glad to see you."

"She never should have run off on me," Gloria said gruffly, going past Rice without so much as glancing his way. "We were friends and friends should always stick together."

"Did you fetch the medicine?" Rice asked Fargo.

"I did."

"Good. Carson has taken a turn for the worse since you left. He's in a bad way. I don't rightly know if he'll last out the day."

One look confirmed the assessment. Carson was on his back, by the fire, bundled to the chest in two heavy blankets. His face was coated with perspiration, his skin unnaturally pale, and his lips quivering as he stared blankly at a patch of blue sky visible through the tall trees.

Shirley sat by his side, using a moist cloth to dampen and cool his brow. She turned to take the leather pouch from Fargo and sadly shook her head. "He's burning up inside. I'm no doctor, but I think he has lead poisoning."

Fargo knelt to examine the young man for himself. He'd seen more gunshot wounds than he cared to count, and he'd had to learn quite a bit about mending those who got shot up. What Easterners and greenhorns alike didn't know was that more people died of complications from bullet wounds than died on the spot when they were shot.

Lead poisoning, in fact, was more common than most folks realized, and Carson was showing all the symptoms. In addition to his pallor and fever, blue spots showed on his gums, he couldn't lift his arms on his own accord, and every so often he convulsed lightly.

"Damn," Fargo muttered, sitting back on his haunches.

"What can we do?" Shirley asked urgently.

Fargo beckoned her to join him and walked a few yards off so the young man couldn't hear. "Give him some laudanum for the pain. Toward the end he won't have much feeling in his body so it won't matter by then."

"We can't cure him?"

"No. Even the best doctor in the world couldn't do a thing at this point."

"He's so young."

"If a man's meant to drown, he'll drown in a desert."

She gave him a sharp look and placed her hands on her shapely hips. "Skye Fargo! I never thought I'd hear you talk so cruel. How could you?"

"It's a saying the cowpunchers down Texas way have," Fargo explained. "It just means that a man will die when he's due to die, and there isn't a damn thing he can do about it."

Shirley's indignation faded. "Well, in any event, we sure can't go off and leave Carson like this. We have to stay until . . ." she said, and stopped, unwilling to complete the sentence. After a few seconds she remarked, "Thanks for bringing Gloria along. Did she give you much trouble?"

"Not at all. It was her idea. She said she missed you."

"Really?" Shirley declared, pleased at the news. She stared at her friend, who had dismounted and was hovering over Carson. "She's tough as nails outside, but inside she's soft. I hope I can convince her to room with me when we get to Denver."

"She's lucky she made it here," Fargo mentioned. "She was so drunk I didn't think she could stay on her horse, but somehow she did."

"Gloria drunk? That'll be the day. Why, I've seen that woman down three bottles of whiskey in the span of an hour and never bat an eye."

Fargo chalked the statement up to exaggeration and stepped toward the pinto. "Since you have everything well in hand, I'm leaving for a while."

"Again? Can't you sit still for a moment? I swear you must have ants in your britches."

"There's work to be done," Fargo said, forking leather and starting to swing the Ovaro toward the trail.

"Wait!" Gloria exclaimed, whirling, suddenly aware he was about to depart. "What's this? I thought we'd share some coffee and relax for a while."

"Some other time," Fargo replied.

"Please!" Gloria insisted.

Shaking his head, Fargo rode from the stand of aspen, gave a wave to Rice, and bore to the east. He figured Carson would linger for up to eight hours, no longer, which was plenty of time for him to accomplish what he had in mind and get back before dark.

The stallion flowed effortlessly over the ground, its long mane flying. Fargo pulled his hat down tighter so the wind wouldn't sweep it off his head and adjusted his body to the rhythm of his mount. Standing out clearly, the wagon ruts led him mile after mile until he came to the crest of a ridge and far below saw the outlaws making their way through a lush valley.

Fargo shucked the Sharps, verified there was a cartridge in the chamber, and sought the cover of forest to the north. Narrowing the gap, he drew abreast of the wagon to note the positions of the riders. Three rode in front, two at the back, and all five were now carrying their rifles. A chunky man in black pants appeared to be in charge in Traute's absence.

As Fargo rode on ahead to get in front of them, he wondered about Ringald. The gunman hadn't been at the ranch. Nor had there been any trace of him in town. Where had he gone?

A mile farther on, the trail wound between two low hills, and it was there that Fargo decided to make his stand. He audaciously rode into the open, right into the middle of the trail, and sat waiting, the Sharps in the crook of his left elbow. Picking the outlaws off from ambush would be less risky, but he had never been branded a bushwhacker, and he wasn't about to become one now.

Overhead a majestic bald eagle soared on the air currents, its mighty wings outstretched. To the left a marmot shuffled out of its burrow, spied the intruder on the horse, and whistled its shrill warning for the benefit of its plump cousins.

The lead riders came into view, then the ore wagon and the rear guards. Someone shouted and pointed at the opening between the hills. The man in the black pants, bellowing an order, raised an arm and the procession ground to a halt.

With the eye of a seasoned frontiersman, Fargo had picked his spot well. Three hundred yards separated him from the band, three hundred yards of flat, open ground. He saw the outlaws conferring together and draped the rifle in his lap so he could adjust the sight. Then he took a bead and waited for them to charge.

Only they didn't charge.

The man acting as their leader gave his rifle and his revolver to a companion, hoisted his hands high so Fargo could see he was unarmed, and rode forward.

What were they up to? Fargo asked himself, lowering

the Sharps. They must recognize him, even at that distance, and he'd counted on them rushing headlong into the sights of his rifle in their eagerness to put an end to him once and for all. Now this. He let the chunky rider draw within ten yards, then said, "That's close enough, mister. And keep those hands touching the sky unless you want a new navel."

"Will do, Trailsman," the man said. "My handle is Boelter. I came to parley, not get myself killed."

"I'm listening."

"My pards and I figure you're not going to let us pass. You aim to kill us and take the wagon."

"You boys are downright brilliant, but you've only got it partly right."

"How so?"

"I don't give a damn about the ore."

Boelter blinked, then cleared his throat. "Listen, Fargo, we didn't have anything to do with what happened to you in Serenity and puttin' you to work in the mine. That was all Traute's doing. You know how he is."

"Get to the point."

"The point is this." Boelter's elbows sagged an inch. "What if we were to turn and just ride off? Would you let us go in peace?"

"Go where?"

"Anywhere except back to Serenity. Denver, maybe. We've all been hankerin' for a taste of city life."

"You're headed there anyway."

Boelter shifted in the saddle and frowned. "I'm being honest with you. Hell, none of us likes working for Vincent Traute anymore. He thinks he has the right to ride roughshod over us, and he treats us like dogs. I don't suppose you heard that he had poor Jeeter hanged?"

"I heard."

"Then what do you say?" Boelter asked, his elbows sagging another inch. "We've never done you any harm."

The Trailsman glanced at the wagon, debating whether he dared trust them, and saw only three men on horseback. The fourth horse was riderless. Where had the man gone? Suddenly he found out, as the outlaw abruptly rose from the grass a hundred yards away and snapped a rifle to his shoulder. In a flash Fargo realized his mistake; he had failed to keep a careful eye on the others while Boelter approached and kept him talking.

The realization came a heartbeat too late, because the next instant the rifleman fired.

13

Fargo owed his life to the outlaw's poor marksmanship. The bullet nipped lightly at his shoulder, and then he was in motion, throwing himself to the right to put the Ovaro between the rifleman and himself even as he leveled the Sharps at Boelter, who had drawn a concealed revolver and was taking aim at his chest. In midair he fired, the Sharps thundering in his ears, the stock recoiling painfully into his side.

The heavy slug struck Boelter in the chin, ruining the lower half of his mouth and blowing out a fist-size hole in the back of his head.

Fargo hardly noticed when Boelter fell. He was busy reloading the Sharps, his fingers flying, as he stood to see what the other outlaws were doing. The rifleman was running toward him, while the three men on horseback had spread out and were rushing to enter the fray. Quickly he took a bead on the rifleman, held his breath to steady the barrel, and squeezed off his shot just as the rifleman was getting set to shoot. The man flipped backward into the grass.

Yells of rage and curses rose from the throats of the three riders, and they opened fire even though they lacked a clear target.

Fargo heard slugs thud into the ground close to the pinto, sparking him to spring swiftly into the saddle, yank on the reins, and race into the shadowy gap between the hills. He didn't want one of their wild shots to hit the stallion. Jamming the rifle into its scabbard, he rode until he was in the open and cut sharply to the left, riding up the gradual, brush-covered slope of the hill to the top.

Far off the wagon was in full flight, heading for Serenity, clouds of dust trailing in its wake. The three outlaws were much closer, almost to the gap.

Fargo reined up, but not before one of the outlaws spotted him and shouted a warning to the others. Three rifles were trained on the crest, and three shots sounded a lethal chorus. Hornets buzzed the air. Fargo promptly wheeled the stallion and rode down the opposite slope, across an open space, and into the forest.

He was furious at himself. How could he have been so stupid? Everything that could go wrong had gone wrong, and all because he hadn't stayed alert. Maybe he simply wasn't thinking straight. He had been on the go for so long, with so little rest and nourishment, it was taking its toll on his mind and body.

Turning westward, he rode rapidly after the fleeing wagon. He may have been thwarted once, but he'd be damned if he was going to let that ore get safely back to Traute. Within minutes a loud racket south of him indicated he was close to his quarry. Accordingly he angled through the pines until he laid eyes on the bearded driver, who was applying a whip to the team and cursing, both with equal energy. Again and again the man glanced apprehensively over his shoulder.

Fargo drew his Colt but didn't show himself as yet. Soon the wagon came to a grade, and the driver worked the whip even harder, goading the horses to the top where he hauled on the reins to bring the wagon to a rattling stop. Lifting a rifle, the outlaw stood and turned in his seat.

Fargo was close to the edge of the trees but well hidden by intervening branches. He noticed that beyond the wagon there appeared to be a drop-off of some kind. Raising his voice, he called out, "Drop that gun or die!"

Startled, the driver spun toward the forest, then froze with his weapon half raised. His beady eyes darted right and left, but he was unable to spot Fargo.

"Drop it!"

The man frowned, hesitating for the time it took him to appreciate his fate should he resist. Then he angrily tossed the rifle to the ground and slowly elevated his arms. "It's done, mister! Don't kill me!"

Emerging, Fargo rode up to the wagon and cocked his revolver. The driver glanced at it and nervously licke his lips.

"I did as you wanted. There's no need to shoot."

"You want to live, I take it?"

"Who the hell doesn't?"

"Some of your friends didn't back yonder."

The driver mustered a wan grin. "We should all be thankful for the fools of this world. Without them none of us would be worth a hoot."

Keeping the Colt trained dead center on the driver's torso, Fargo moved around the back of the wagon to the far side. The man shifted so as not to lost sight of him. Dismounting, Fargo backed up to the edge of the drop-off and looked down. Forty feet below lay scattered boulders.

"What do you have in mind, mister?" the driver asked suspiciously.

"I want you to turn the wagon this way, then climb down and unhitch the team," Fargo instructed him.

"If you're fixing to do what I think you're fixing to do, I should tell you here and now that Vincent Traute ain't going to like this. He'll have you sliced into pieces and fed to the varmints."

"Do it."

Mumbling to himself, the driver sat down, picked up the whip, and moved the wagon in a tight loop, stopping when the horses were mere yards from the rim and the wagon was aimed directly at the drop-off. He hefted the whip as if contemplating whether to use it, then set it aside.

"Get down," Fargo ordered. "And don't bother with the brake."

The man dutifully obeyed. He gazed toward the two hills, clearly hoping his fellows would come to his aid.

"The team," Fargo reminded him, and stood close by while the man removed the horses from harness and gave them smacks on the rumps so they would move off out of harm's way. Once all the animals had been freed, Fargo nodded at the long tongue that was lying on the ground. "Raise it," he said.

"By myself? It's too heavy for one man to lift."

"Try."

"I can't, I tell you."

"What was that you were saying a while ago about fools?" Fargo asked harshly. He knew the man was stalling, and he knew why. The driver reluctantly stepped to the tongue, placed his hands underneath, and lifted, the single-trees rattling and swaying as he raised the tongue high enough to be swung back against the front of the wagon where it came to rest with a thud, jutting skyward like a barren tree. Puffing, the driver moved back and rubbed his hands together. "There," Fargo said, "that wasn't so hard after all, was it?"

"Now what?" the man demanded.

"Lift your shirt."

"Do what?"

Fargo wagged the Colt. "You heard me. Quit your damn stalling." The man was wearing an old homespun shirt that hung loosely down to well past his hips. There might be a belly gun hidden under there, and Fargo wasn't about to make the same blunder he had with Boelter.

The driver complied, exposing a hairy belly and nothing else. "Satisfied?"

"Now start walking," Fargo said, motioning toward the hills. "Tell your friends not to bother going back to Serenity unless they're looking to be planted three feet under."

Parting his lips to respond, the driver apparently thought better of the idea, clamped his mouth shut, and whirled. Fists clenched, he stormed off.

Fargo had to move rapidly, before the other gunmen arrived. He slid the Colt into its holster, then removed his lariat from his saddle, adjusted the loop, and, with a single overhand swing and a flick of his wrist, roped the wagon, sending the loop over the brake handle. This was a mountain wagon, specifically made to transport heavy loads over rugged terrain, with a California rack bed, rear wheels more than four feet high, and a larger than normal brake handle needed to slow the wagon on steep mountain grades. The rope settled around the base of the handle.

He moved in front of the tongue, took up the slack, and dallied the rope twice around his saddle horn. Using his legs, he urged the pinto forward. The stallion took a single step, then was brought up short by the rope. "Keep going, big fella," Fargo coaxed and was rewarded when the Ovaro threw itself into the effort with all the power it could muster. Its steely muscles rippling, its head lowered, the pinto moved first one leg, than another. Slowly the wagon budged, creeping a few inches forward.

"That's it," Fargo offered encouragement, his legs slapping the stallion's sides. "A little more and we'll be there."

The Ovaro nickered, threw its shoulders again into the attempt, and covered a yard. Behind them the wagon rattled a bit faster. "More," Fargo said. He saw the front wheels complete a revolution. The tongue shook but didn't fall. Once more the wheels turned. Now the wagon was inching toward the rim of its own momentum. Gravity was taking over and doing a better job than the pinto could do.

With a jerk of his arm, Fargo snaked the rope loose and pulled it up and off the brake handle. He moved aside and stopped to coil his lariat, watching the ore wagon rumble to the edge of the drop-off, gaining speed each second. A victim of its own momentum and massive weight, the wagon simply rolled off the rim and plummeted from sight.

The crash, seconds later, was tremendous.

Fargo had to hold tightly onto the reins in order to keep the Ovaro under control. Shying skittishly, it started to make for the pines, prancing and bobbing its great head. "Whoa, boy," he said softly, patting its neck. "Whoa, there."

Seldom did the pinto fail to do as he wanted. Years of enduring untold hardships together had bred an abiding trust in both horse and rider, so unlike mounts that gave free rein to their fears at the least provocation. The Ovaro heeded his every wish even in the face of the gravest dangers. Now the big stallion quieted and let itself be guided to the brink of the drop-off.

Shattered pieces of ore and broken sections of wood littered a wide area. The bed of the wagon was partially intact, but the tongue had split into huge jagged splinters on impact and all four wheels were broken. Repairing the wagon would be impossible. If Traute wanted to get more ore to civilization, he must first purchase a new wagon.

Fargo hoped he would be there to see Traute's face when the son of a bitch learned about the loss. Reattaching the lariat to his saddle, he prepared to ride westward when from the bottom of the grade there came the pounding of rushing hoofs. He just reached the cover of the forest as the three outlaws swept onto the top and abruptly halted.

Riding double with one of them was the driver. He pointed at the spot where the wagon had stood when he walked off, and said something. They moved to the dropoff. The sight that greeted them provoked a torrent of heated swearing.

Hidden in the trees, Fargo waited for their decision. If they rode on eastward, he would allow them to leave in peace; if not, he would stop them then and there. They were Traute's pawns, third-rate outlaws of no consequence in the scheme of things, but if they returned to Serenity, they would make the job he had to accomplish that much harder. His palm curled around the butt of his Colt.

"What do we do now?" one of the riders asked.

"We go back to Serenity and tell Traute," said the man who was riding double with the driver.

"And have him hang us like he did Jeeter?" said the third rider.

"That mangy Trailsman said we should skedaddle if we know what's good for us," the wagon driver commented. "Me, I ain't about to run from any man. I don't care how high and mighty he's supposed to be."

"You're saying we should go back?" inquired the first rider.

"I don't know about you, pard, but I've never tucked my tail between my legs and slunk off from a fight before, and I'm not about to start now," the driver declared.

They exchanged looks. As one, they turned their horses to the trail. As one, they reined up when the broad-shouldered figure in buckskins appeared out of the pines and blocked their path.

"Son of a bitch!" one of them blurted.

Skye Fargo eyed each of them, his hand still resting lightly on his Colt, waiting for one of them to make the first move. The rider on the right was blinking nonstop. The one on the left had his hand poised to draw, but his face exposed the fear that prevented him from clearing

142

leather. It was the man in the middle, the one riding double with the driver, who would be the fool who started the gunfight, Fargo decided. The outlaw had the crafty aspect of a weasel and was wearing the smug smile of someone who thought he was invincible. Skye Fargo had met such idiots in the past, men who believed they lived under a lucky charm that always spared them from harm. Others might fall, but never them. They believed they would live to a ripe old age. And ten times out of ten they were wrong.

Growing tired of waiting, Fargo goaded them with a casual "Well?"

The man in the middle went for his gun, his action serving as the signal for his companions.

Fargo's right hand leaped up and out too swiftly for the human eye to follow. His thumb and forefinger worked the hammer and the trigger with blinding speed, his three shots blasting the three riders into eternity. And then, for extra measure, as the wagon driver vainly tried to yank the middle rider's rifle out of the saddle scabbard, he fired a fourth time, giving the driver a new nostril.

The Trailsman's gunshots rippled out over the valley to the twin hills and eventually died on the wind.

Fargo peered through the gunsmoke at the bodies, then methodically reloaded the Colt. He had achieved what he set out to do, striking his second serious blow against Vincent Traute. But there was a lot left to do. His next move would be against the ranch. Serenity he would save for last.

First, though, he must see about Shirley and the others. He replaced the Colt, gathered up the horses and the weapons of the dead men, checked the contents of the various saddlebags, and headed for the stand of aspens. There were now more than enough horses, guns, and provisions to see the women and the former prisoners safely to Denver if they didn't become lost along the way.

Out of necessity he took his time getting back to the aspens. He had a long string of horses to lead, and he knew that trying to gallop with so many in tow would result in snarled rope, collisions, and possibly broken legs. So he didn't reach the stand until the afternoon was on the verge of evening. Well before he arrived, however, he beheld a sight that caused the short hairs at the nape of his neck to prickle as if from a heat rash.

A column of whitish gray smoke was curling upward from the refuge.

Fargo saw the smoke from over a mile off and straightened in alarm. What in the hell were they trying to do? he angrily wondered. Give their location away? They might as well stick out a sign telling Traute where they were. Shirley and Rice should know better than to build a fire that big.

Then worry set in. Shirley and Rice did know better; they wouldn't be so brainless. But if they hadn't made the fire, who had? A dozen questions flashed through his mind, and although he had the answer to none of them, he was filled with foreboding. He brought the Ovaro to a trot and hauled roughly on the lead rope so the string would keep pace.

When still two hundred yards from the aspens, Fargo left the trail and took the horses into the woods. Sliding down, he tied the stallion and the spare mounts to trees, then pulled the Sharps and glided Indian-fashion toward the spiraling smoke. He smelled the acrid odor long before he actually saw the stand.

He stopped and crouched at the border of the clear space ringing the hideaway, and suddenly his eyes narrowed. There, lying half in the aspens and half out, was a bloody body. He scoured the vegetation on all sides but detected no movement. There might be outlaws lying in hiding to ambush him, so he waited, listening and looking until he was as sure as he could be that those who attacked the stand were no longer there.

Taking a breath, he shoved to his feet and ran a zigzag pattern to the body. There were no shots, no shouts. Dropping to one knee, he grimaced on seeing the fifteen to twenty bullet holes in the dead man's back. He didn't need to roll the body over to know who it was. Rice had been shot to ribbons.

Rising, he silently entered the aspens and had gone only a few yards when he found the second body. This time it was Yost, flat on his back, half of his face blown away and a score of crimson holes dotting his chest and abdomen. Both men, Fargo reasoned, must have been taken completely by surprise and gunned down before they could so much as blink.

A bitter bile formed in his mouth as he moved inward. The slender trees had been chipped and nicked by countless slugs, and some were spattered with Yost's blood. Farther in he spied the fire itself, greedily devouring the last of a huge pile of branches. Close by was a third body.

Fargo glanced to the right and the left, then padded up to Carson. The young man lay as still as stone, but amazingly he didn't bear a single gunshot wound. His face was ghostly white. As Fargo leaned forward to feel for a pulse, Carson abruptly opened his eyes.

"It's you! I thought they had changed their minds and come back to finish me off," he said weakly.

"Traute and his men paid you a visit." Fargo stated the obvious, putting his hand on the younger man's forehead. Carson was burning up alive, his skin blistering to the touch.

"Caught us flat-footed."

"How did they find you?"

"They had help," Carson said and suddenly broke into violent convulsions, his legs jerking up off the ground and his shoulders shaking uncontrollably. The fit persisted for over a minute.

Fargo placed his hands on the man's forearms until the shaking subsided. Carson, he knew, hadn't much time. He must find out what happened before it was too late. "Feel up to more talking?" he asked.

"Do my best," Carson whispered and licked his lips.

"What did you mean by Traute had help?"

"It was Gloria. She tricked you, tricked all of us."

"How?"

Carson's eyelids drooped, but he managed to rouse himself. "Traute had put her up to having you bring her to Shirley. He figured you'd show up in Serenity. Told me so himself. Gloated on it, in fact, after Rice and Yost were dead."

Fargo had seldom felt such intense hatred as now washed through him.

"Gloria waited till Shirley and those two were talking at the edge of the stand," Carson went on softly. "Then she heaved limbs on the fire, making it bigger and bigger,

145

as a signal so Traute would know right where to find us." Tears formed in his eyes. "I had dozed off and was sleeping. The next thing I knew, I woke up and there were flames shooting five feet high. Gloria was laughing like a crazy woman. I tried to yell, to warn the others, but I was too weak." He paused. "It was too late anyway. Traute had figured we were hiding somewhere outside the valley, so he was waiting near the gorge with his men for Gloria's signal. They were on us in no time."

"I found Rice and Yost. What happened to Shirley?"

"Traute took her. Told me to tell you that if you want to see her again, you should go to his ranch. Said he'll be waiting for you."

"I won't disappoint him."

"He won't be alone."

"I know."

"I wish there was something I could have done," Carson said forlornly. "Do you know what? The bastard didn't finish me off because he didn't want to waste a bullet. Those were his exact words." His voice wavered. "God, I want him dead!"

"He will be soon. I promise."

"Shoot him once for me," Carson said and without warning broke into convulsions again, this time more violently than before, his whole body thrashing and bouncing as his mouth opened in a silent scream of agony and despair. He gurgled and whined, then gasped and blurted, "I wish . . . I wish . . ."

"Yes?" Fargo said, feeling totally helpless.

But the final yearning of the young man would never be known. Carson went limp, exhaling loudly, and locked his eyes on Fargo. A last tear welled up at the corner of his eye, and he died.

Fargo reached out and gently closed Carson's eyelids. Inwardly he was a seething cauldron of rage. He slowly rose and faced due west. "All right, Traute," he said under his breath. "You want me. Here I come."

14

The Rockies were bathed in the pale glow of the unblinking moon when the Trailsman spotted the cluster of buildings that were Traute's headquarters. They were all as dark as the night, as ominous as a pit filled with vipers. In and among them waited human rattlesnakes who would stop at nothing to put an end to the Trailsman's career.

He knew what he was letting himself in for, yet he never slowed. Had people observed him, they would have seen a big man sitting loosely in the saddle, relaxed and unconcerned, as if he was going to visit a close friend instead of a bitter enemy. Unless people could see into the depths of his soul, they would have no idea of the killing fury that gripped Skye Fargo.

But he wasn't reckless. Sixty yards from the buildings he drew rein and dismounted. He tied the reins to a convenient bush, and then he doubled over and advanced at a brisk run, palming the Colt along the way. He made for the corral, intending to work along it to the barn and from there to the house.

A pinpoint of orange light flared in the night, close to the ground at the bottom of the corral. Fargo immediately dived into the high grass. Someone was in the corral, smoking a cigarette. He figured it was an outlaw who had grown bored waiting for him to show up. The man had decided a few puffs couldn't hurt, but to play it safe he had flattened so the cigarette couldn't be seen from afar. The ruse had almost worked. If Fargo hadn't been approaching from just the right angle, he might have missed the glow.

He saw it flare again, then diminish as the outlaw took a drag and exhaled. Crawling forward, quietly parting the grass with his forearms as he advanced, he drew within thirty feet of the corral. He couldn't see the smoker, but he knew where the man was lying from the position of the cigarette. Taking careful aim at a spot two inches above the orange glow, he thumbed back the hammer.

Just then, from the barn, a surly voice hissed, "Jones, you asshole! Put that damn thing out! He might be here at any minute!"

Fargo fired. The shot was greeted by a strangled cry, and the cigarette fell to the ground. Then the night erupted with gunfire. One man cut loose from the barn, three others from the house, all aiming at the point where they had seen the Colt's muzzle flash.

But Fargo was already in motion, rolling to his left for eight feet and rising to sprint to the end of the corral. One of the gunmen glimpsed him, and slugs tore into the wooden fence, sending chips flying. Fargo crouched and waited for the firing to stop. Just within the corral lay a sprawled inky form, beside it the smoldering cigarette.

Keeping low, Fargo moved along the corral, closing on the rear of the barn. The gunman had been at the front. Fargo saw that the hay doors were wide open and made out a rope hanging from a pulley. Pausing, he gripped the top rail and vaulted over the fence. The Colt went under his belt. In a burst of speed he reached the rope, and started his way upward. Hand over hand he climbed to the hay doors.

Once in the loft he froze and strained his ears. From below came the patter of footsteps as someone moved from the front of the barn to the back. The gunman was now directly underneath him, probably scanning the corral. He drew the Colt but didn't cock it yet. A minute dragged past. Then he heard the outlaw move toward the front of the barn again.

Taking small steps, Fargo inched to the end of the loft. He halted well short of the edge so none of the loose hay would tumble onto the floor below and give his presence away. The open front doors were in deep shadows, preventing him from spying the gunman.

At that juncture, from up at the house, came a hail. "Jones! Nesbit! Did we get him?"

There was no answer. The man below, who must be Nesbit, was no fool; he knew Fargo was still alive, and he wasn't going to advertise his location by answering the hail.

"Jones? Nesbit? Are you there?"

Fargo tilted his head. That last person had sounded like Marshal Ward. Even now Traute was trying to make things nice and legal. If Ward and these others killed him, Traute could later claim they had just been doing their job in tracking down and slaying an escaped criminal. He bent low and probed the darkness for Nesbit.

A rustling noise drew his attention to the right side of the great doors. A patch of black moved against the backdrop of shadow. Seconds later the outline of a head poked out past the jamb, silhouetted by the patch of lighter colored earth outside. Nesbit was now surveying the area in front of the barn. Elevating his right arm, Fargo took a bead on the back of the gunman's head. He gave a low whistle, saw the head swing around, and squeezed off his shot.

Nesbit staggered backward into full view, his arms flailing the air. He toppled onto his back, tried once to rise, and went limp.

Guns roared at the house. Bullets smacked into the side of the barn, causing some of the already skittish horses in the stalls to neigh and plunge. None of the slugs came anywhere near the Trailsman.

Fargo had the outlaws in the house worried and knew it. He replaced the spent cartridges in his Colt and shoved the pistol into his holster, then climbed down the ladder to the floor. One by one, starting with those nearest the rear wall, he went to each of the stalls and freed the horses. But he didn't allow them to leave until he had them all gathered in the center aisle. Then, with a wave of his hat and a loud shout, he stampeded them out the door. As the last animal swept past, he leaped astride it.

The horses were scattering in all directions, so it appeared perfectly natural for the one he was controlling to slant toward the house. He covered half the distance, then heard an irate bellow.

"Here he comes! He's on that damn horse!"

Shoving off, Fargo hit the ground close to a bush and scrambled behind it as the outlaws blasted away. The animal he had been riding, hit repeatedly, whinnied in pain. It floundered along for a half dozen yards, then crashed down onto its side and slid a good dozen feet. The outlaws continued to shoot, their slugs smacking into the poor creature like rain onto a metal roof.

Fargo hadn't counted on that. He hadn't meant for the animal to suffer. Rising to his knees, he saw a gun flash from an open window to the left of the front door and answered with two swift cracks of his Colt. Another gunman was just inside the door, the third at a window on the right. Now both directed their shots in his direction.

He spun and jogged to a water pump, dropping behind it while the dirt around him was chewed up by bullets. Suddenly the firing stopped. The outlaws were reloading. He took advantage of the lull to crawl hurriedly from the pump into a patch of weeds adjacent to the side of the house.

The gunman at the door fired twice more, his rounds pinging off the metal pump.

Then the night was as still as a tomb.

Skye Fargo reached the side wall and crouched. Moving to the back, he peeked around the corner and discovered a single closed door about in line with where the front door was. Working swiftly, he fed fresh cartridges into the Colt. The momentary respite gave him his first chance to think in minutes. He realized there hadn't been so much as a peep out of Traute, nor had there been any sign of Ringald. Were they deliberately lying low and letting the underlings do all the fighting? Or was there another explanation for their absence?

He held the Colt close to his chest, the barrel slanted upward, and glanced at the back door. As yet no one had opened it to check the rear of the building. The outlaws, he hoped, still believed he was somewhere out front.

Taking a breath, he sprinted to the door and halted with his back to the wood bordering the jamb. A metal latch afforded entry, but was it locked? Gingerly he touched the latch and pressed ever so lightly. It resisted for a moment and he thought he would be thwarted. Then, slowly, the latch moved. He continued to apply just enough pressure to lower it; if he went too fast, the latch would give off a loud click and alert the men inside.

Fargo felt his palms sweating and wished he could

wipe them on his leggings. The latch reached the bottom of the vertical groove, but he could tell it had not sprung the lever. Some latches were more stubborn than others and had to be worked up and down before they worked properly. He dared not do so.

Controlling his impatience, Skye pressed a bit harder and was rewarded by feeling something give inside. The door eased inward a fraction of an inch. He put his thumb on the revolver hammer and took a deep breath. Now was the moment of truth. If they knew he was there, he was as good as dead. If not . . .

He gave the door a mighty shove and swung into the doorway, ducking low as he leveled the Colt, and instantly spied a figure between him and the open front door, a figure that was turning toward him with a gun in its hand. His Colt boomed twice, the impact flinging the figure into the front doorway where the man was outlined for the briefest instant before toppling over, and in that instant he recognized the phony lawman, Marshal Ward. Then he dived to the right just as a gunman at the window cut loose with three swift shots that slammed into the wall above him. From a prone position he returned fire twice and saw the gunman twist, clutch at his chest, and fall into the window, shattering the glass in the upper pane.

Fargo could hear his blood pounding in his ears as he scooted to a table and flipped it over for cover. Hugging the floor, he began reloading. The interior of the house was unnaturally quiet; no other shots punctuated the darkness. He finished filling the cylinder, then rose on his left knee and peeked around the tabletop. Nothing moved. Outside, someone groaned.

Was that all of them? he wondered. What about Traute and Ringald? The groan was repeated. Rising, his every nerve on edge, he moved to the front door and surveyed the barn and the fields. If there were more outlaws around, they weren't advertising the fact.

A third groan almost at his feet compelled him to hunker down and sidle out to Ward. The so-called lawman, his arms outflung, had his eyes wide open.

"Fargo?" he croaked.

He made no reply.

"I know it's you," Ward rasped and coughed once.

"You're a regular hellion, mister. Ain't never seen the like."

Off to the northwest a few horses were moving. Otherwise, all was calm.

"I think you broke my back," Ward was saying. "I can't hardly move."

"Where's Traute?"

"Likely sitting in the saloon in Serenity waiting for us to show and tell him you were taken care of." Ward laughed bitterly. "Afraid he's in for a nasty shock."

"And Ringald?"

"Ain't seen much of him, come to think of it. He should have been here with us. Maybe then we'd have stood a prayer." He paused. "Damn. I think I'm bleeding inside, too."

Fargo shifted, looking from one end of the house to the other. He wasn't yet entirely convinced he had disposed of all the opposition. Until he was, he'd remain vigilant.

"We should have killed you the minute we found out who you were," Ward said. "Cutler was right all along. You're the meanest cuss on two legs when you get your dander up."

"I'll give Traute your regards," Fargo said and began to slide toward the door.

"Wait!" Ward blurted, a note of panic in his tone.

"What?"

"Don't leave me like this."

"There's nothing I can do for you," Fargo said.

"Like hell there isn't. You can put me out of my misery."

"No."

"You'd shoot a lame horse, wouldn't you?"

"You're no horse. And I don't owe you any favors," Fargo noted, moving his right leg.

"Please!" Ward said. "You can't up and leave me lying here like this! I could lie here for days before the end comes, and I'd rather get it over with now than have to go through all that suffering."

"No one twisted your arm and forced you to work for Traute. You made your bed; you lie in it."

"Please!" Ward begged, and then added quickly,

"How about a trade? You agree to do as I want, and I'll give you information I'm sure you'd like to know about."

"No deals."

"You don't want to hear about all the money Traute has?"

Fargo was almost to the doorway when the mention of the hoard stopped him and he glanced back. He didn't want Traute or any of the other outlaws profiting from their blood money, and he would do everything in his power to ensure they didn't. "I'm listening," he said.

"You'll put me out of my misery?"

"You won't have to suffer," Fargo promised.

Ward smiled gratefully. "Traute has the money with him. He was afraid to leave it here. Carries it in four big satchels he bought in Missouri a few years back. He's never told us how much he has, but I'd guess it's over a hundred thousand dollars. Maybe more."

"You haven't told me much I hadn't already guessed."

The hardcase took that as a change of heart and bleated, "You gave me your word! You just said I wouldn't have to suffer."

"Can you move your fingers?"

"What? Barely," Ward answered. "Why? What difference does it make? I can't move my arms or my legs."

"It makes all the difference in the world," Fargo said. He had seen Ward's pistol lying nearby, and he now picked it up and squatted next to Ward's right hand. Placing the grip against Ward's palm, he closed each of the outlaw's fingers, sticking the forefinger through the trigger guard so it rested on the trigger. Then he aligned Ward's arm so that the tip of the barrel was a fraction of an inch from the man's ear. Finally he cocked the six-shooter. "There. All you have to do is squeeze."

"But I wanted you to do it for me."

"I promised that you wouldn't have to suffer," Fargo said, stepping to the doorway. "I never promised to do the job for you. If you have the gumption, squeeze. If not, quit your bellyaching."

Ward was silent for a moment. "You're a hard man, Trailsman."

Fargo, entering the house, saw a lantern on a small table by the left-hand window. He had lifted the glass and was striking a match to light the wick when the house thundered to one last gunshot.

In the spreading glow he discerned a comfortably furnished room. Vincent Traute had spent a hefty sum to make the house a home. He examined the two bodies to be certain the hardcases were dead, then went into the pair of bedrooms and collected lanterns from each. A check of the kitchen cupboards revealed a can of kerosene, which he opened and liberally sprinkled all about the room—on the rug, over the furniture, even on the drapes.

At length he took the extra lanterns outside, then went back in, held the lit one aloft, and smashed it down onto the rug. Instantly flames shot up. Black smoke billowed. He backed out, retrieved the lanterns, and made for the barn.

As he lit the two lanterns, loud crackling and hissing came from the house, where the interior now blazed like the sun, the flames dancing in the windows and licking up the sides of the front door. Smoke poured from every opening.

Fargo carried the lanterns into the barn and over to the hay loft, examining the stalls as he went by to be sure that none of the horses had strayed back inside. With an overhand toss he hurled first one lantern, then the other, into the hay, and stood to watch as it caught fire.

The corral and the area in front of the house were illuminated as clearly as at midday, when he strolled across the field to the Ovaro. Climbing up, he sat and observed the destruction of Vincent Traute's headquarters, seeing both buildings become engulfed in sheets of driving flames that gradually reduced the structures to charred cinders.

Reins in hand, Fargo turned to the northwest, toward Serenity and toward his showdown with Traute.

The only light was in the saloon. Spilling out of the window and the entrance, the glare plainly revealed four saddled horses at the hitching post. Elsewhere shadows reigned; the barn, the marshal's office, the house the two women shared were all invisible from a distance.

Fargo approached from the south, walking the pinto

to avoid riding into a trap. On the mountain a wolf howled. To the east an owl wanted to know who was there.

The livery doors were open wide. As Fargo went past, he faced them so as not to be shot in the back. He did likewise with the marshal's office and the other buildings. But no one tried to gun him down. Random musical notes floated from the saloon as he stopped in front of the bat-wing doors and swung to the ground.

Someone inside was tapping on the piano keys.

Arms at his sides, Fargo stepped to the doors. They were all there: Griswald behind the bar, polishing glasses; Ringald in front of it, sipping a drink; Gloria at the piano, gloomily tapping; while Shirley and Traute were seated at a card table, cards in their hands. The whole scene appeared so normal, so typical of a frontier saloon, but he knew otherwise.

Fargo shoved the doors apart and took three measured strides, putting him about even with the piano, which was on his right. Traute and Shirley sat to his left, close to the bar. The gunfighter and the bartender stood in front of him. Of them all only Gloria stopped what she was doing and glanced up as he made his appearance. If hatred wore a mask, it would be her face.

"Well, hello again," Traute said pleasantly. "We've been expecting you."

Shirley looked at Fargo, her anxiety transparent. She had acquired a nasty welt above her right eye and a bruise on her cheek.

"Now, now, my dear," Traute chided her. "What did I tell you about keeping your mind on our game?"

"Sorry," she responded fearfully.

Fargo concentrated on Ringald. The bantam gunman had placed his back to the bar and had both elbows resting on top, a posture that put his hands mere inches above his twin pearl-handled pistols. Ringald wore a confident smirk.

"I take it that the fire we could see from out front was my ranch?" Traute suavely inquired.

"It was," Fargo confirmed.

"How petty of you. And Marshal Ward and the others? I presume they were unable to offer objections when you burned my place down?"

"You'll need to find someone else to wear a badge for you."

Traute lowered his cards and leaned back. "Easily done, Mr. Fargo." He gazed at the gunfighter. "Ringald, how would you like to be town marshal?"

"Do I get a raise?"

"Two hundred dollars a month and every Thursday night with the woman of your choice for free."

"For that amount I'll wear two badges."

"There you have it, Mr. Fargo," Traute said, smiling expansively. "When you have the money and connections that I do, the world is your oyster." He set his cards down and smoothed his sleeve. "Speaking of which, why don't you sit down here with me so we can discuss our disagreements like civilized men?"

"On your feet," Fargo said.

"Hear me out, please. It will be to your advantage," Traute said. "I'm willing to admit I made a mistake in having you put to work at the mine. And I'm also willing to make amends by offering you fair compensation."

"How much?"

A sly smile curled Traute's mouth. "I knew you were a reasonable man. What would you say to ten thousand dollars? You fill your saddlebags, you ride off, and that's the end of it. You don't notify the army. And you won't ever come back this way, either. Agreed?"

"How about twenty thousand instead?"

"If that's what you want."

"Forty thousand?"

Doubt and something else tainted Traute's voice when he answered, "Now see here, you're trying to blackmail me, and I won't stand for it. Twenty thousand is my top offer. Take it or leave it."

"I'll leave it."

"You'll what?" Traute demanded, shoving out of the chair. "Do you have the foggiest notion what you're passing up? Twenty thousand is more than a lot of honest men make in a lifetime. With that kind of money you can do whatever you damn well please. See something of the world. Go to St. Louis, Chicago, New York. Bed a different woman every night. Everything you've ever dreamed about could be yours."

"The only thing I've dreamed about the past few days is seeing you dead at my feet," Fargo declared.

At last Traute acknowledged the inevitable. He nodded curtly at the gunfighter and said, "As your first order of business, Marshal, I want you to put this man back under arrest and if he resists, kill him."

"With pleasure," Ringald said, stepping away from the bar and easing his hands downward until they were fully extended. "What will it be, Fargo? Drop that hog-leg, go back to work at the mine, and you get to live."

"Go to hell."

Palpable tension filled the musty air. Traute waited breathlessly for the gunplay. Griswald was the opposite, lounging at ease with his fleshy arms folded. Gloria sat riveted in morbid fascination, Shirley in naked fear.

Fargo emptied his mind of all thoughts and held his right hand loose and ready. When the gunman drew he would have a split second to react. And then he would have another split second to deal with Traute and the barkeep because as sure as he was standing there they would try to blow holes in him while his attention was on Ringald.

Gloria suddenly tittered. "Kill the bastard, Ringald, and I'll give you a night you'll never forget."

Fargo noticed that the bantam wisely made no reply. Ringald's total attention was on him. They both had been in enough gunfights to know that a lapse of concentration at the wrong moment meant the difference between life and death. He saw Ringald's jaw muscles tighten, saw the gunfighter's eyes become flinty with resolve, and he inwardly braced for that instant when his life would hang in the balance.

And then several things occurred almost simultaneously.

Without warning Shirley shouted "Hey," and shoved her chair back from the card table with all her strength, causing the chair to tip over backward on its rear legs and crash to the floor. At her outcry Ringald, who had poised his hands for the draw, glanced for a fraction of a second in her direction. So did the bartender, who was making a grab for something under the bar. Ringald then completed the draw, his hands like greased lightning, but the damage had already been done. The distraction cost him dearly.

Skye Fargo's Colt leaped clear of his holster and thundered just as Ringald was bringing his pistols up. The bantam staggered rearward, recovered, and leveled his guns. Again Fargo sent a slug into the gunfighter's chest and again Ringald staggered, a red dot appearing squarely above his heart on his black shirt. Ringald's knees sagged, but he was still game, still deadly, and he lifted his right arm to get off at least one shot before eternity claimed him. Fargo's Colt spat smoke and lead one final time. As if smashed by a hammer, Ringald was flung into the bar and slumped to the floor.

All this had happened in seconds.

Now Fargo had only three unspent cartridges in his Colt, and it was now that the barkeep and Traute played their hands. Griswald straightened from behind the bar, a shotgun in his pudgy grip, while Traute snaked a hand under his jacket and pulled a revolver. Their intent was obvious. They would catch Fargo in a cross fire while he was standing in the open.

But Fargo was one step ahead of them. Or, more precisely, three steps, as he took a running dive for the piano and threw himself to the floor at its side just as the bartender's cannon boomed. Too late, he had seen Gloria rising to get out of the line of fire. Too late, he realized she had done the exact opposite. He felt moist drops splatter his cheeks, saw her fall, and swept to his knees, taking aim over the piano seat at Griswald's stocky form.

A slug from Traute bit into the piano, jangling several keys, and then Fargo fired, his bullet striking Griswald high on the left side. Both Traute and the barkeep disappeared behind the bar, and suddenly the saloon was quiet except for Gloria's pathetic gurgling.

Fargo ducked low and hastily reloaded. A shuffling noise and a single footstep came from the other end of the room. He peered out but saw neither of his enemies. He did see Shirley lying on her side, and he tried to recall if in all the confusion she had accidentally been shot. Flattening, he slowly crawled toward her, using the tables and chairs as cover. When he got close, she abruptly rolled over, winked, and grinned.

He put a finger to his mouth in warning, and she nodded her understanding. Retreating to the table he had just passed, he rose to one knee. What were Traute and Griswald waiting for? he mused. For him to make the first move? He wasn't about to go rushing around the end of the bar into the barrels of Griswald's shotgun. If he had to, he'd wait them out.

Unexpectedly, from out back of the saloon, arose the drumming of hoofs. From the sound, the rider was heading due west, toward the mountain that had indirectly been the cause of so much heartache and sorrow.

Puzzled, Fargo listened intently. He wondered if Traute had posted outlaws at the mine again, and if someone was going to fetch them. But so far as he knew the only ones left were Traute and Griswald. Suddenly he remembered there had been only four horses tied to the hitching post out front. Yet there had been five people in the saloon when he arrived. Where had the fifth horse been?

The logical answer jolted him. He realized Traute had outfoxed him again. Rising, fearful of having Traute escape, he dashed to the bar and threw himself onto the top, sweeping his cocked Colt back and forth in search of a target. His wariness was wasted. Griswald lay in a spreading puddle of blood, blank eyes fixed on the ceiling.

"Damn!" Fargo blurted, dropping to the floor and moving to Shirley's side as she stood. "Traute sneaked out the back door and lit out. I'll have a hell of a time finding him in the dark."

"He's on his way to the mine," she said.

"Why there?" Skye said doubtfully. There was nothing at the mine to interest Traute. If the man was smart—and there could be no denying that Traute was as shrewd as they came—then he was on his way to the gorge right at that moment. The Ovaro, if Fargo hurried, might be able to catch him before he got there.

"He won't leave without his satchels," Shirley said.

"They're at the mine?"

She nodded. "He used to keep them under the floorboards out at his ranch, although none of us knew it until we were getting ready to leave earlier and he pulled them out. I guess he figured Ward might not be able to stop you, and he didn't want to leave his money where you might find it." She glanced at Gloria, who was gurgling louder. "When we were almost to town, he told the others to go on ahead and took me with him up to the mine. He wanted me, but I wouldn't let him so he knocked me down. That's when I saw him carry those satchels of his into the shack. He probably figured they'd be safer there than they would be in Serenity if you showed up."

Fargo had heard enough. Whirling, he ran to the batwing doors and paused long enough to shout, "Stay here until I get back."

"Be careful!"

He vaulted onto the saddle, grabbed the reins, and lashed the stallion into a gallop. Around the north end of town, across the flat stretch beyond, and up the slope of the mountain he rushed, determined to stop Traute from getting away even if he had to ride the pinto into the ground. In his mind's eye he kept seeing Haggerty's face at the moment the old man had removed his leg iron and Carson's face as the young man died. Traute had much to pay for, and Fargo was going to see that he did.

He didn't bother to use stealth. The time factor was too crucial. He had to reach the shack before Traute was able to load the satchels and flee. Colt in hand, he and the Ovaro crashed through underbrush and ducked under low limbs. The pinto was breathing heavily, winded from its strenuous exertions, when he burst from the woods and spied the shack and the cabin ahead.

Traute's horse stood in the pale moonlight in front of the shack. The outlaw leader appeared in the doorway, two satchels over each shoulder. He glanced at Fargo, then ran for his mount.

Fargo snapped off two hurried shots in an attempt to drive Traute back into the shack where he could keep the outlaw pinned down. In that he was unsuccessful, but something even better happened. The bullets clipped the grass near the roan's front hoofs, startling it so badly that it shied, spun, and raced off to the north.

"No!" Traute roared, his six-shooter out. For a moment he seemed about to fire at his horse. Then he pivoted, banged off a wild shot at Fargo, and turned on his heels to run toward the coal black maw of the mine.

Fargo angled into the shelter of the shack and leaped down. Moving to the corner, he caught a glimpse of

Traute as the man vanished inside the shaft. Crouching, he gave chase, covering less than ten yards when the flash of gunfire drove him to the ground. Traute, concealed in near total darkness, had the edge.

Fargo slowly worked his way on a diagonal course toward the mine. He thought to check his cartridge belt to be certain he had plenty of ammunition, and as his fingers roved over the leather loops, he heard his name called.

"I know you can hear me," Traute went on. "Answer me. We have to talk."

Since responding would give his location away, Fargo kept silent and continued crawling.

"This isn't a trick, damn you!" Traute bellowed. "I can make you a rich man. All you have to do is listen to me and agree to my terms. What do you say?"

The tinge of desperation in the outlaw's voice made Fargo smile as he continued working his way toward the right side of the tunnel.

"Why won't you say something?" Traute called shrilly. "I promise not to shoot. You have my word."

Fargo would rather trust an Apache on the warpath.

"I'm a rich man, Trailsman," Traute said, speaking urgently as if he sensed Fargo was closing in and knew his time was running out. "I have four satchels here filled with the proceeds from ten years of operating this mine. Think of it! Over one hundred thousand dollars and I'm willing to share it with you. Half is yours if you'll turn your back and let me ride off. Do you hear me?"

Now Fargo was near enough to make out a vague figure standing just inside the mine on the left side. The temptation to shoot was well-nigh irresistible, but he realized he might miss, and he wanted to be dead sure when he squeezed the trigger.

"Are you deaf? Doesn't that much money mean anything to you? You'll be set for life!"

Ten yards was all Fargo had to go. He reached out his left hand, then began to slide his right leg forward. His knee hit a stone, which rolled a few inches, rattling lightly. It was all Traute needed to pinpoint him. The night rocked to gunfire, and two slugs smacked into the dirt inches from his head. He replied in kind and saw Traute run deeper into the shaft.

Pushing up and doubling over, he darted to one side of the opening and crouched with his back to the rock wall. He heard the dull thud of boots within, then they stopped. Putting his eye to the edge, he tried to find Traute, but it was a hopeless cause. The tunnel was blacker than black. Not even a mountain lion would be able to see in there.

Fargo saw a bright flash and felt rock chips pelt his face. He jerked back as the shaft reverberated to the report of the gun. How Traute had seen him, he had no idea. Just to give the outlaw hell, he held out his arm, tilted the Colt so that the barrel was pointing in Traute's general direction, and fired. The din of the blast, amplified by the confines of the tunnel, was deafening.

"Damn you!" Traute roared.

Faint footsteps signified the polecat was going deeper. To hurry him along, Fargo fired again. The answering shot was much fainter than before. Then there came a low rumble, resembling thunder at a great distance, and a panicked shout.

"Wait! No more firing! The roof is crumbling!"

"Oh really?" Fargo said to himself. His features hardened as he poked the Colt out once more and thumbed back the hammer. "For Haggerty," he said, his finger curling around the trigger. This time the rumbling grew louder, almost as loud as Traute's shrill shriek.

"No more! I give up! I'm coming out!"

Fargo guessed that the outlaw was fifty feet or better from the entrance. "For Carson," he said grimly and fired again. With more rumbling the air inside the shaft filled with fine particles of dust.

"Stop, for God's sake!" Traute wailed, the words barely audible.

"And this one is for me," Fargo stated grimly. He let the hammer fall, and it was as if the entire mountain came crashing down. The ground under his feet shook. The rumble became a tremendous, earsplitting crash, like an entire case of dynamite going off all at once, and the roof of the mine collapsed, raining down tons of dirt and rock. A billowing cloud of dust exploded out of the mouth of the tunnel, engulfing Fargo, sweeping down over the slope. He threw himself to one side and hunkered down, barely able to breathe, until the cloud dissipated.

Gradually the din subsided.

Two minutes passed before Fargo could safely stand and walk to where the opening had been. A solid wall now barred entry, sealing the silver vein for all time and burying the man who had dared to enslave his fellows in the name of rampant greed. Skye Fargo turned his back on the filled shaft, twirled the Colt into his holster, and walked toward the pinto with a new bounce in his stride.

Three hours later they reined up short of the gorge and looked back at the west end of the valley where a towering sheet of flame consumed the timbers and planks that had gone into the construction of the seven buildings.

"Sweet Jesus!" Shirley said. "The whole damn town! I can't believe it." She paused. "Now I know why you said we didn't have to bury Gloria."

Skye Fargo glanced at the three horses she was leading, all piled high with her personal effects. "Are you sure you brought enough?"

"I had to leave the furniture, didn't I?" Shirley retorted. "And you can't expect me to start my new life in Denver buck naked." She tugged on the lead rope. "You'd just better hope none of these critters come up lame, or you'll be carrying my stuff back."

"Like hell I will." Fargo entered the gorge, feeling weary to his core and looking forward to the stop he planned to make in a couple of hours so he could catch up on his sleep before pushing on to the southeast. He commented as much.

"Why wait till daylight, handsome?" Shirley asked, lowering her voice seductively. "We can find us a nice spot yonder and cuddle the whole night through."

"Not tonight."

"Why? Are you planning to take priestly vows sometime soon?"

"I'm tired, woman. Can't you see that?"

"I swear! I've never met a man so uninterested in sex in all my born days," Shirley groused and recoiled in surprise when the Trailsman threw back his head and laughed loud enough to be heard clear to Denver.

163

LOOKING FORWARD!

**The following is the opening
section from the next novel in the exciting
TRAILSMAN series from Signet:**

THE TRAILSMAN #139
BUFFALO GUNS

*1860, Western Kansas Territory—
a lawless tract of horizon, grass, and sky
where some men grab what they want when they want it—
other men's buffalo skins, money, or women . . .*

The warrior sprawled on the buffalo grass and stared wide-eyed into the blank blue sky above. The afternoon sun gilded the bronze skin of the dead Indian's face. His mouth sagged open as if he could not believe his own death. A headband, its eagle feathers askew, was tangled in the brave's long dark hair. The ragged hole of the bullet wound darkened the buckskin shirt, and the handle of a tomahawk protruded from the bloody shoulder.

The tall man sat astride the black-and-white pinto and gazed down at the body. His lake blue eyes slowly and methodically scanned the scene before him, noting the trampled buffalo grass, the Indian's clothing, the wounds. Slowly he shook his head, then glanced up at the wheeling hawks. The vultures would come in soon.

Skye Fargo regarded the dead man again. And he heard, inside himself, the voice that recited what he knew about what had happened. Fresh blood—a fresh kill. The brave had been dead less than an hour. The beaded moccasins—white with distinctive jagged triangles and stripes—marked him as Cheyenne. And the number of eagle feathers were a sign that he had been a respected warrior. The wide bullet wound indicated point-blank range.

Fargo dismounted and knelt on the ground for a moment, examining the coarse, trampled sod. The matted grass was too thick to make out a clear track. But the bent and broken blades showed signs of a struggle. He followed the tracks and found the faint traces of several horses. Fargo frowned and walked back to the body, stooping over it to examine, at last, what disturbed his mind the most.

He yanked the stone tomahawk from the flesh of the warrior and wiped the blood off on the grass. Then he held the tomahawk before him and took the emblem, which dangled from a buckskin thong, between his fingers. The disc was fashioned of buffalo leather, painted yellow with a blue circle in the center. It was a miniature of a war shield. And it was Kiowa.

Skye Fargo shook his head again, puzzled.

"Kiowa," he said out loud to himself slowly. "Killing Cheyenne." It didn't make sense. Kiowa had upheld the tribal treaty for twenty years. Back in 1840, the two southern tribes—the Kiowa and the Comanche—had come north of Arrowpoint, which is what they called the Arkansas River, to hold a big powwow with the Cheyenne and Arapaho. The four tribes met, exchanging horses and gifts and promises of peace. And they had kept the treaty. At least until now. If the tribes started fighting one another, it would be only a matter of time before a white man was caught in the cross fire. Then the killing would spill over to the settlers, too. And Cheyenne and Kiowa were some of the fiercest warriors on the plains.

Fargo held the tomahawk in his hand and examined it again. It was carefully made. The smooth mesquite wood handle fit snugly around the chipped quartz blade. Yucca cord wrapped the grip handle, carved in curves to fit the hand. It was a fine weapon. Fargo raised it into the air and brought it down, whistling through the air—beautifully balanced.

The axe had not killed the Cheyenne brave. The bullet

had. And the tomahawk had been left in the Indian's shoulder. No Indian would abandon this, Fargo thought, hefting the tomahawk again. Such weapons took many months to perfect. Indian warriors always conserved their weapons. Fargo had seen them pull arrows from game and from dead men in order to repair and use them again. The Kiowa who owned this tomahawk had been in a hurry, Fargo thought. Or wanted to leave a message for anyone who could read it.

Fargo stowed the tomahawk in his saddlebag and remounted the pinto. He gazed eastward across the waving tawny grass. A half a mile away, a line of white bones striped the rolling plain. Fargo had passed by the spot before he discovered the dead Cheyenne. More than thirty bison killed in one place. White hunters. It was getting to be a common sight on the Kansas prairie.

Beyond the white buffalo bones the horizon was sharp against the September blue sky. Several miles back, still out of sight, the wagon train was following. He had led the supply train out from Independence, Missouri, along the Santa Fe Trail through Council Grove and Fort Dodge before leaving the trail and driving parallel to the Arkansas River to Fort McKinney. It had been an unremarkable trip, Fargo thought. Until now.

He glanced at the lowering sun and calculated how much daylight he'd have once the wagons caught up with him. If he pushed their pace, the wagons would arrive at Fort McKinney just after nightfall, a day earlier than expected.

Fargo decided to search for tracks before he rejoined the wagons. He took the pinto in an ever-widening spiral around the dead Indian. Soon he found what he was looking for.

Indistinct horses' hooves again. And two deep lines of torn sod—the trail of a travois—traveling north to south, heading toward the Arkansas River.

Now what was the Cheyenne brave, or his killers, hauling on a travois? Fargo chewed on that question as he galloped back to the wagon train.

The dozen clapboard buildings comprising Fort McKinney clustered around a wide and dusty parade ground on a gentle bluff overlooking the Arkansas River. Like most forts in the west, it didn't have a wall around it and had never been attacked. Instead, it served as a staging base for military operations in the surrounding countryside.

In the five years since the fort had been established, a town had sprung up around it, attracted by the comforting prospect of military protection. The collection of sod houses and yellow lumber buildings sprawled chaotically on the riverbank.

The last red of the autumn sunset was fading to purple as Fargo brought the wagons to a halt in front of the quartermaster's storehouse. A skinny private, just a kid, scurried forward, clicked his heels and saluted smartly.

"Where's the quartermaster?" Fargo asked. Before the kid had a chance to answer, a grizzled second lieutenant emerged carrying a lantern. Fargo dismounted and handed over the requisition order.

"I'll need to check the supplies against the list before I can pay you," the lieutenant said. "Army regulations. Going by the book."

They had never held him up to take inventory before. Fargo started to protest, then thought better of it. "While you're doing that, where's Colonel Straver? I need a word with him."

Fargo and Colonel Straver went way back. Straver was one of the few military men Fargo respected; he was disciplined, forthright, and sensible. But he was also a man who hadn't lost his independence after a long career in the military. It would be prudent to alert the colonel about the dead warrior he had seen on the prairie. If the peace between the Kiowa and the Cheyenne was about to be broken by full-scale war, then Straver would want to know about it.

"Gone," the quartermaster said absentmindedly as he perused the list of supplies.

"Where?"

"Hm?" The lieutenant glanced up. "Oh, yes. The colonel has gone west with the troops to follow those renegades who have been jumping the stagecoaches south of Denver City. They won't be back for two weeks. There's hardly anybody left here at Fort McKinney."

Fargo bit his lip in thought. Troops gone for two weeks. If the Cheyenne and the Kiowa launched into a full-scale war, even against each other, there would be a panic in the town. If things got bad, the commanding officer at the fort would have to organize the townsfolk to protect themselves. That would take some real leadership.

"Who's in command?"

"Major Brimwell," the quartermaster answered. He looked up at the line of fifteen wagons. "Major Brimwell is the reason I have to go by the book here." Fargo heard the impatience in the lieutenant's voice. "Otherwise, I'd just pay you and be done with it. In any case I'll be finished inventory here in about an hour," he said. "You'll find the major in the officers' quarters."

"Fine," Fargo said. "The wagons are yours, except the last one over there." Fargo pointed to a wide-bodied mountain wagon filled with wooden crates.

The lieutenant nodded. "Just out of curiosity, what's in it?"

"Petticoats," Fargo said with a smile. "Lace petticoats and things like that. Hundreds of 'em."

The quartermaster chuckled.

"You must be doing a job for the Gilded Cage."

"Yep," Fargo said. "Can't beat the pay." He moved off toward the officers' quarters. He was thinking of Sylvia. After he had spoken to the commanding officer, he would make his delivery to the Gilded Cage—and then enjoy his reward.

A smile of anticipation still lingered on Fargo's face as he crossed the threshold of the officers' quarters and found Major Brimwell at a card game with several officers.

The major threw down his hand as Fargo approached.

"I'm having no luck tonight," he complained. "Who are you, sir? What brings you here?"

"I brought in the supply wagons," Fargo said, taking an empty chair at the major's elbow as they watched the game finish. "I need to talk to you."

The major rose and ushered him into a small bare office. Brimwell took a seat behind the desk and poured two shot glasses of bourbon, sliding one across to Fargo.

"I saw something ten miles east of here you should know about," Fargo said.

"Ten miles east?" the major repeated. "At Reggio's Trading Post?" Fargo thought of the hunchbacked trader, Reggio, and his lively trading post on the river. After his business here and at the Gilded Cage, Fargo had to pay a visit to Reggio to deliver the cash payment he was carrying in the inside pocket of his coat.

"No," Fargo said. "Not on the river. North of there a few miles, on the prairie. I found a dead Cheyenne—"

"So?" Brimwell cut in impatiently. He poured himself another shot and downed it. "What's one more dead savage?"

"He'd been shot at close range. And he had a Kiowa tomahawk embedded in his shoulder."

The major glared across the desk at Fargo. "You interrupted my card game, sir, to tell me that?"

Fargo shrugged. The man was stupid—and without curiosity or imagination. Brimwell was everything Fargo hated about the military. Follow the rules. Don't ask questions. Don't use your brain. That's what military life did to some men. The weaker ones, anyway. The stronger ones, like Colonel Straver, were tempered by it, hardened like fine steel that never lost its edge. But Brimwell was not one of those.

"A Kiowa tomahawk in a Cheyenne brave," Fargo repeated slowly, trying to summon patience and keep his temper in check. "Those two tribes have had an unbroken treaty for twenty years. And now there might be war between them."

The Major leaned forward.

"Now I understand, sir," he said, thumping the table with his knuckles. "That's wonderful news! If the Kiowa and the Cheyenne are going to butcher each other, it will save us a hell of a lot of time. Much faster than finding the provocation to kill those redskins ourselves. This is the best news I've heard since I've been out here in this godforsaken country. Indians slaughtering Indians! I'll drink to that!" The major poured himself another shot and refilled Fargo's glass. He clinked his glass to Fargo's, which sat on the desk, before draining his.

"Wonderful news," he said, wheezing.

Fargo watched the Major. Stupid. Damn stupid, he thought—the kind of man who didn't see danger coming straight at him, until it was too late.

"There's something else," Fargo said. He didn't like Major Brimwell. And with every passing moment he liked him even less. "No Kiowa would leave a good tomahawk in an enemy's shoulder—unless he's in a hurry to get away, or he wants to leave a message."

The major shrugged. "That seems to me a petty detail, sir," he said. "Nothing to concern yourself with. Indians leave their weapons all over the place. All over the place." The major's voice was slurred from the bourbon—his reasoning, too.

"No," Fargo said slowly. "They don't. There's something very strange about this to my way of thinking."

"Why there's nothing strange at all," Brimwell said. "One barbarian slays another. Nothing strange . . ." The major hiccuped loudly. "I'd say, sir, that the only thing strange is your way of thinking. In fact, I'd say you think mighty strangely. You think, sir, like an Indian!" The major hiccuped again.

"I guess I do," Fargo said, rising to leave. "I guess I do at that."

It was his fifteenth and final trip through the crowded bar of the Gilded Cage. The wagon was nearly unloaded. Fargo balanced a wooden crate on his shoulder. Petticoats were surprisingly heavy.

"Mr. Fargo!" the bartender called as he passed by.

Fargo paused, resting the crate against the bar. The bartender leaned across and spoke low.

"What?" Fargo called out, not catching the man's words. "It's noisy as a calf corral in here!"

The bartender leaned closer until he spoke into Fargo's ear. "Somebody's been asking about you." Fargo nodded, and the bartender's large, watery eyes blinked a few times.

"What about me?"

"Wanted to know what your name is. Let slip he'd heard you were coming into town with wagons. Real surprised to find you here. Said he expected you'd be in tomorrow. He asked one of the girls, and she didn't like his tone. She just told me while she was getting him another drink."

Fargo nodded again. "Which one is he?"

"Sitting over against the wall by the door," the bartender said, careful not to point or to let his watery eyes stray in that direction if the man happened to be watching. "The one with the big fur cap on. Looks like a mean son of a bitch."

"I'll look him over," Fargo said. "And I'll watch my back. Thanks for the tip."

The bartender turned to another customer, and Fargo lifted the crate onto his shoulder again. He made his way to the staircase and climbed halfway up. Then he turned, as if tired, and rested the crate against the banister. He wiped his forehead with one sleeve as his eyes swept the room.

The Gilded Cage was jammed with customers, standing at the bar, playing cards, and drinking at the tables. Fargo noticed a familiar figure at the piano. He'd have a talk with Mandy later.

Just as he turned back, he let his eyes sweep the wall near the door. The man was there all right—he lifted the crate and continued up the stair—an ugly burly bastard with a thick brown beard and a tattered fur cap, sitting alone next to the door, back to the wall. A man didn't usually take that position unless he was planning to cause some trouble and make a quick escape. And he'd been watching Fargo. His beady black eyes had been fixed on him as Fargo's gaze passed him by. On the other hand, it could be nothing, Fargo thought. But he knew the man was up to no good. He'd get to the bottom of it later, but first, a more pleasant task. He climbed the final stair.

He could hear their voices all the way from the other end of the hall. He made his way down the papered corridor and pushed open a door, entering and depositing the crate onto the floor. The room was a blizzard of lace, crinoline, and frills. Fluffy piles of petticoats, most of them white and all of them ruffled and flounced, covered the chairs and sofas of the drawing room. He bent down and pried the top off the last crate.

"Oh, Skye you darling!"

A pert brunette named Bernadette flung her arms around him when she saw the pink lingerie in the last crate, and other girls squealed and gathered around. Fargo gave Bernadette a squeeze, enjoying her soft curves. She kissed him quickly and wriggled from his grasp to kneel beside the newly opened box. In a moment the air was a fountain of flying lace as she pulled the undergarments from the crate and tossed them about the room to the other girls.

So many girls ran about in various stages of undress that Fargo had a hard time counting them all—maybe fifteen, he concluded. And all of them, every single one, was screeching with delight. Fargo covered his ears and uttered a complaint, but no one heard him above the din.

He kept his hands over his ears and watched as a curvaceous redhead, packed into a tight lavender corset that pressed her large breasts upward, struggled out of a bright yellow petticoat. A willowy brunette sitting on a horsehair couch extended one long leg and slipped her pointed toe into a red garter, pulling it up onto her slender thigh. She glanced up, noted Fargo's appreciative gaze, and smiled back. But her attention was distracted immediately by a plump blonde modeling an extravagantly lacy petticoat that billowed about her. Fargo turned away and descended the stairs, his ears ringing. He wondered where Sylvia was keeping herself.

As he descended the staircase, out of the corner of his eye Fargo saw the man beside the door come slowly to his feet. Fargo flexed his right hand, ready to turn and draw. He continued down, but the man simply stood, not making a move. By the time he reached the floor, the man was out of sight again, hidden by the crowd standing at the bar. He'd have to keep an eye out.

All the tables were filled. Some of the girls had already come downstairs, and Fargo was amused to see that their skirts were vastly inflated by an extravagance of petticoats underneath.

Fargo glanced around the jammed room but didn't see Sylvia anywhere. Fargo ordered a beer from the bartender.

"I saw him," Fargo said as he paid. "Anybody know him?"

"I asked a couple of the other girls," the bartender said. "Nobody's seen him around here before."

"He's a buffalo hunter, by the looks of him."

"And a mean one," the bartender said, nodding.

Fargo took a swig of the beer and searched his memory for the man's face. He was sure he had never seen him before. If he was following Fargo, he had probably been sent by somebody else. But who? And why?

Fargo turned to look out at the crowd. Mandy was still the piano man. He pushed his way to a chair beside the battered upright piano. Mandy glanced over at him, then smiled broadly in recognition, his white teeth bright in his black face.

"Why Mr. Fargo," Mandy said. "Miss Sylvia didn't tell me it was you bringing those underthings for the ladies. I should have known it."

Mandy's big hands moved faultlessly over the black and white keys.

"How have you been, Mandy?" Fargo said. He glanced toward the door again. He could see over the heads of the men sitting at the tables. He was still there. Still standing against the wall. Still watching.

"Never better."

"And business?"

"I guess you haven't heard the news," Mandy said, shaking his head in mock sorrow, trying to suppress his smile. "Miss Sylvia, she's been doing better than ever. Making so much money, she hardly knows what to do with it. 'Cept now she's got that all figured out."

"And what's that?"

"Why she's closing down the Gilded Cage, at the end of the month. She's buying a ranch up Nebraska way. And I aim to work on it. That's why she's been buying all those things for the girls, to set them up right. Some of 'em are getting hitched. Some of the others will continue gaming, I reckon. It's a sad thing, closing down the Gilded Cage."

"It's a terrible thing," Fargo agreed. "I'll bet there's a lot of serious mourning going on over at Fort McKinney. But where is Sylvia? I haven't seen her yet."

"Oh, she's around," said Mandy swiveling his head.

Just then a door opened to the side of the bar. Fargo stood up as a small figure emerged. Wearing a flamboyant red dress with two red ostrich feathers crowning her head, Sylvia Roland, the Silver Sparrow, made her grand entrance.

She was small, hardly bigger than a half-grown girl, but roundly shaped. Her ash blond hair fell in perfect ringlets down her back, and her dress was cut low to reveal a creamy neck and two beautifully rounded breasts above a tiny waist. Fargo watched as the bartender hoisted Sylvia onto the bar. She got to her feet and walked the length of it, stepping gracefully over the glasses and bottles. Her fringed skirt was cut to reveal her slender ankles and her red leather laced boots. She paused to chat and laugh with the men at her feet. They toasted her as she made her way to the end of the bar and back.

She spotted Fargo immediately and let out a yell. The bartender swung her down, and she quickly bustled over to the piano.

"You're here at last!" she said as Fargo bent over to kiss her. Her mouth was as sweet as honey, as sweet as he remembered, and he felt her surprisingly strong arms reach up to embrace him. Fargo grinned and lifted her off her feet.

"Put me down!" she said, pretending to struggle in his embrace. "What will my customers think?"

Indeed many of the men sitting at the tables around the piano had turned to watch them—and with barely disguised envy. The Silver Sparrow made it a rule never to cavort with the customers. The sole exception was Skye Fargo.

Fargo's eyes flicked toward the door. Still there. Still watching.

"They'll think we haven't seen each other for a long time," Fargo said, nuzzling her fragrant hair. He held her with one arm only. His other hand hung loose, near his Colt.

"And that's the truth," she said. "But later. Put me down. I have to maintain some kind of dignity." Fargo grinned. He turned and hoisted her on top of the piano, turning around again quickly. The man beside the door hadn't moved.

"You can't come down until you sing," Fargo teased. The tables around them fell silent as the customers scraped their chairs against the wooden floor so they could see better. Several voices called out excitedly for a song from Sylvia. Then a hush fell on the room.

Just as Mandy struck the opening chords, there was a sudden movement beside the door. Fargo leaped aside as the bullet whizzed by him. Piano wire twanged as it hit the upright. Fargo swept Sylvia off the piano, pushing her onto the floor where she'd be out of the line of fire. The men at the bar scrambled for cover under the tables.

Fargo turned and drew as a second shot exploded. Mandy cried out and slumped down, crashing onto the keyboard, a dark bullet wound in his back.

Fargo felt rage swell inside him, a fury so deep it darkened the room until he saw only the brown-bearded bastard standing beside the door, pistol raised, preparing to fire again. Everything moved in slow motion as Fargo raised his pistol, noting the man's beady eyes and thick brow. Fargo squeezed the trigger, catching him in the shoulder. He wanted to keep the man alive so he could get a few answers out of him.

The man recoiled and his pistol fired again, the shot flying wide. His pistol dropped from his hand. Fargo continued to advance, Colt raised. The brown-bearded stranger saw him coming. Fear blazed in his eyes as he clutched his wounded shoulder. His gaze darted to the floor where his pistol had fallen. Suddenly he threw himself onto it, scrambling to get hold of the weapon with his good hand. Fargo had reached him and grabbed him by the collar when the man's pistol went off.

The body jerked with the impact, then relaxed.

Fargo swore and rolled the body faceup. The shot had caught him dead center in the chest. The face was slack, eyes lifeless. Fargo swore again. He would get no answers out of this one.

Suddenly Sylvia was beside him, tears streaking her face. She clutched at Fargo's arm.

"Who would want to kill . . . to kill Mandy?" she sobbed. The room began to buzz as the customers got to their feet again and gathered around.

"I don't know," Fargo said, looking down at the man lying before him. An innocent man was dead, and the murderer could answer no questions.

Fargo knew the bullets had been intended for him. He had no doubt of that. But for the moment, as he looked around the crowded room, he'd keep his thoughts to himself.